YOUR DAD WILL DO

A TOUCH OF TABOO NOVEL

KATEE ROBERT

TRINKETS AND TALES LLC

ALSO BY KATEE ROBERT

Wicked Villains
Book 1: Desperate Measures
Book 2: Learn My Lesson
Book 3: A Worthy Opponent
Book 4: The Beast
Book 5: The Sea Witch
Book 6: Queen Takes Rose

The Island of Ys
Book 1: His Forbidden Desire
Book 2: Her Rival's Touch
Book 3: His Tormented Heart
Book 4: Her Vengeful Embrace

The Thalanian Dynasty Series (MMF)
Book 1: Theirs for the Night
Book 2: Forever Theirs
Book 3: Theirs Ever After
Book 4: Their Second Chance

The Kings Series
Book 1: The Last King
Book 2: The Fearless King

The Hidden Sins Series
Book 1: The Devil's Daughter

Book 3.5: His to Take

Serve Series
Book 1: Mistaken by Fate
Book 2: Betting on Fate
Book 3: Protecting Fate

Come Undone Series
Book 1: Wrong Bed, Right Guy
Book 2: Chasing Mrs. Right
Book 3: Two Wrongs, One Right
Book 3.5: Seducing Mr. Right

Other Books
Seducing the Bridesmaid
Meeting His Match
Prom Queen
The Siren's Curse

To every person on Twitter and Instagram that responded to with YES, DO IT. I did it, and it's for you.

CHAPTER 1

JANUARY

*H*ow does one go about seducing their almost-father-in-law? I really, truly do not recommend doing an internet search. The results are heavy on porn and light on answers. In the end, I'm left to my own devices.

That's how I end up on his front porch in a short black dress and thigh-highs in the middle of January, well after the polite hours of visiting. I'm shaking as I knock on the door, and it's not purely because the icy wind makes my clothing feel like a laughable barrier.

Despite the late hour, he's awake. My breath catches in my throat as the door opens to reveal him. Shane. The man who, up until a few days ago, was supposed to be my father-in-law. Funny how quickly things change when you least expect it. Or not so funny at all. I sure as hell don't feel like laughing.

He fills the doorway, a large man with broad shoulders, big hands, and a smattering of salt and pepper in his hair. He's in his late forties, some twenty-ish years older than me. Shane frowns as recognition slips over his handsome face. "Lily? What are you doing here?"

"I was hoping we could talk." I have to clench my jaw to keep my teeth from chattering. Maybe I should have gone with the trench coat route. At least then I'd have a coat.

To his credit, Shane doesn't make me wait. He moves out of the way and holds the door open so I can walk past him. The first blast of warmth makes me shiver again. Maybe if I hadn't stood out there for so long, gathering my courage, I wouldn't be so cold now.

"What did he do?"

I blink and stop trying to rub feeling back into my fingertips. "Excuse me?"

"My asshole son. What's he done now?" He catches my hand and lifts it between us. My ring finger is markedly empty. Shane skates his thumb across the bare skin, still frowning. Now my shivers have very little to do with temperature and everything to do with desire.

It's yet another indication of the many ways that my relationship with Max wasn't operating on all cylinders. His freaking father can do more with a single swipe of his thumb than Max was ever interested in doing with his entire body. Then again, Max and I only ever had polite, friendly sex—which was *not* what I found him doing with his secretary when I showed up unexpectedly at his office. It's not what I suspect he was doing with the others I suspect came before her.

I don't want to get into it right now. I've already had four days of tears and raging with my girlfriends, but if I start talking about how I found Max fucking his secretary like the biggest goddamn cliché in existence, I'm going to start crying again.

That's not why I'm here.

I'm here for revenge—and maybe a little pleasure, too, though the pleasure rates a distant second in priorities.

"Shane." I say his name slowly. In all the time I dated Max,

I called him Mr. Alby. A necessary distance between us, a reminder of what he was to me—only ever my boyfriend's father. I rip down that distance now and stare up at him, letting him see the pent up emotions I've spent two long years ignoring and denying.

I've spent two long years ignoring a whole lot.

Shane's dark eyes go wide and then hot before he shutters his response, locking himself up tight. But, almost as if he can't resist, he swipes the pad of his thumb over my bare ring finger again. "Tell me what happened."

"We're over." My voice catches, and I hate that it catches. "No going back, no crossing Go, no collecting two hundred dollars. Really, really over."

He nods slowly and then gives my hand a squeeze. "Sounds like you could use a drink."

"I could use about ten, but one's a good place to start." At least he isn't kicking me out. That's a good sign, right? I follow him to the kitchen and watch as he opens the liquor cabinet and picks through the bottles.

He barely glances at me. "Vodka, right?"

"Yes." Of course he remembers my drink. I bet, if pressed, he also remembers my birthday and a whole host of other details that slip past most people, including my ex.

But then, Shane isn't most people.

Heat melts into my bones as he methodically puts together a drink for each of us. I don't know what to do with my hands once I don't need them for warmth, and the coziness of the temperature is a vivid reminder of just how little I'm wearing. My dress is barely long enough to cover the tops of my thigh-highs and while I'm wearing a garter belt, I have nothing else on beneath the thin fabric of the dress. I'm dressed slutty and downright scandalous and Shane has barely looked at me since I walked through the door.

That won't do. That won't do at all.

He finishes with the drinks and I gather what's left of my courage and close the distance between us, sliding between him and the counter to reach for the glass. Just like that, he's at my back, his hips against my ass. "Thank you," I say over my shoulder.

He inhales sharply, but doesn't move back. "What are you doing, Lily?"

His lack of retreat gives me a little more strength. Just enough to sip the drink and then turn slowly to face him. I have to lean back over the counter to meet his gaze, and a thrill goes through me as he forces *me* to make the adjustments. He might as well be made from stone. I tip my chin up. "I have a question."

"Ask it."

"Last summer, you and Max were supposed to be working, so I was here at the pool." I can barely catch my breath. "No one was around so I didn't bother with a suit."

"Mmm." The barely banked heat in his gaze is back, flaring hotter by the second. He still hasn't moved, either to press against me or to retreat. "That's not a question."

I lick my lips. "It felt wicked to be out there naked, knowing I was in your house even if you weren't here. I..." This part's harder, but his nearness gives me a boost of bravado. "I started touching myself. I felt like such a little slut, but that made it hotter."

He's breathing harder now, and he reaches around me to grasp the counter on either side of my hips. "Why are you telling me this?"

"Because it's not anything you don't already know," I whisper. "You were upstairs. I saw you watch me through the master window." I reach behind me to the counter just inside his hands. The move arches my back and puts my breasts almost within touching distance of his chest. "I didn't know you were there when I started, but once I knew you were

4

watching me, I took my time and dragged it out. I wanted you to watch. I wanted you to do more than watch." The last I've never admitted to myself, let alone out loud, but it's the truth. "Do you remember that?"

He exhales harshly. "You don't know what you saw."

"Okay." I'm shaking like a leaf. "My mistake."

Shane still doesn't move away. "Even if I came home for lunch unexpectedly that day, you were dating my son." He shifts forward the barest amount, closing in on me. "It would be fucked up if I stood in my master bedroom while you fingered that pretty little pussy. I'd be a monster to have watched the entire thing and fucked my hand while I pretended it was you."

"Shane," I say his name like a secret, just between us. "I'm not dating your son right now."

"What did he do?"

"I don't want to talk about it."

He shakes his head slowly. "You came here with a purpose, but you don't get to throw yourself at me without sharing the truth. Out with it, Lily. What did Max do?"

I really, really don't want to talk about it, but the sheer closeness of him makes my verbal brakes disappear. I find myself answering without having any intention of doing so. "He slept with his secretary. I think he wanted me to catch him. Either that, or he's just really shitty as hiding it when he's up to no good." Except that's not the full truth, but admitting that I think he's been cheating on me for months and months feels lke admitting that I'm a fool. What kind of fiancé just swallows the lies whole and doesn't question it when things don't quite line up?

Apparently the kind of fiancé that I am.

He curses softly. "I'm sorry."

"I'm not." It's even the truth. I will cry and I will grieve for the future I thought would be mine, and I sure as hell will spitefully fuck Max's dad, but I'm not sorry I avoided tying my life to someone who never should have been more than a friend. Someone who didn't hesitate to hurt me instead of sitting me down and telling me how unhappy he is. Max is selfish and if I wasn't entirely happy in our relationship either, I didn't go out and fuck other people when we were together.

But, as I told Shane just now, we're not together any longer.

I lift myself onto the counter, putting us at nearly the same height. The move has my skirt rising dangerously, flashing my thigh-highs and garters.

Shane looks down and goes still. We both hold our breath as he shifts one hand to bracket my thigh and traces the point where my garter connect with the stockings. "Lily." This time, when he says my name, he sounds different. Almost angry. "If I push up your skirt, and I going to find your bare pussy?"

The words lash me and I can't help shivering. I lick my lips again. "If you want to find out, I won't stop you."

"Dirty girl." He snaps the garter, the sting making me jump. "You came here for revenge."

There's no point in denying it. "Yes."

"I'd have to be a selfish asshole to take advantage of you when you're like this." But he's looking at me in the way I've always fantasized about, like he has a thousand things he wants to do to my body and hasn't decided where he wants to start.

"It's what we both want, isn't it?" When he doesn't immediately answer, I press. "Why *not* do it?"

He moves his hand to my hip and grips the fabric of my dress, pulling it tight against my body. "I could think of a few reasons. You were going to marry my son."

I can't quite catch my breath. "I'm not going to now."

"You're young enough to be my daughter."

I watch the dress inch up my legs with every pull of his hand, baring more and more of me. The sight makes me giddy. It's the only excuse for what slips out in response. "Should I call you Daddy, then?"

He goes still. Just like that, he releases my dress and the fabric falls back to cover most of my thighs. Disappointment sours my stomach, but he's not moving back. He skates his hand up my side barely brushing the curve of my breast before he grips my chin just tightly enough to hurt. "Is that what you want, Lily?" He presses two fingers to my bottom lip and I open for him. "You want to call me Daddy while I do filthy things to you that you've only fantasized about." He slips his fingers into my mouth, in and out, in and out, miming fucking. I watch him with wide eyes, but I don't get a chance to decide if I like it or not before he clamps his remaining fingers tightly around my chin, his fingers almost deep enough to gag me.

Shane leans down and holds my gaze as his fingers stroke my tongue. "You want to call me Daddy while I slip my hand up your skirt and find out what you have waiting for me? While I bend you over this counter and eat your cunt until you come?" It's almost too much, I can't quite catch my breath, I really *am* going to gag, but he gives me no relief. "You want to ride *Daddy's* cock?"

7

CHAPTER 2

$\mathscr{I}$ make a panicked sound and he releases me, sliding his fingers from my mouth. It feels dirty and wrong and I'm shaking with need. "Yes," I whisper. "Yes, that's what I want."

He searches my face. Maybe he thought he'd scare me off with all that, but instead I'm even more turned on. My hands drop to the hem of my dress. "Would you like to see?"

He looks around as if realizing where we are for the first time. "Not here." The kitchen faces the front of the house, and with the lights on, it's only the maple trees in the front yard that keep the neighbors from seeing us.

I hop off the counter and stagger after him on knees that feel like Jell-O. Oh my god, is this really happening? Did I really challenge him like that and now he's called my bluff? Daddy kink is *not* on my list of things I wanted from Shane, but I can't deny that every filthy sentence he spills makes the heat in my blood pulse hotter.

I want to be bad, to be dirty. I want to forget every bit of the last few days. I know the forgetting won't last forever, but at this point I'll take what I can get.

I expect Shane to take me upstairs, but he stalks to the living room with its big sectional couch and square ottoman. When it's pushed together, it basically creates a massive bed, and I've always wanted to fuck on it, but Max was never interested in anything resembling public sex. I watch Shane push the ottoman tight against the couch, my heart beating too hard.

He considers me for a moment and then drops onto the couch and situates himself against the back of it with his big legs stretched out. Like this, there's no missing the way his cock presses against the front of his pants. He crooks his fingers at me. "Take off your shoes."

After a short silent debate, I stand on the ottoman and walk to him. But when I move to straddle him, he shakes his head. "No. Turn around. Lie down." When I don't immediately obey, he moves me how he wants me. Urging me onto my stomach facing the television, my shins and feet bent up against the back of the couch. It feels strange and awkward and it's made worse by the fact we aren't touching.

He must sense my confusion, because he rumbles out a laugh as he takes the remote and puts a movie on. "You don't remember this."

It's only when the opening credits of a bullshit action movie start that I go still. "I was lying between you two like this."

"Yes." He tosses one of the throw blankets over my lower half and then nudges my legs wider. "Just. Like. This." And then his hand is there, burrowing under the blankets and sliding up to bracket my inner thigh. "You were wearing a skirt nearly as short as this. Were you hoping he'd finger you right in front of me?"

Embarrassment and desire twine through me. "Maybe." My breath catches in my throat as his hand shift higher, his rough palm against my bare skin. I swallow hard. "Maybe I was hoping you'd do it."

"Shameless," he murmurs. "Let's see how shameless, shall we?" He yanks the throw off with his free hand and tosses it aside. "Pull up your dress, Lily."

I reach drown and grip the hem of my dress, inching it up over my ass, baring me from the waist down. "Like this?"

"Good girl." He tightens his grip on my thigh. "Spread your legs and lift your hips." As I obey, his hand shifts higher and cups my pussy. We both exhale shakily. I expected him to jump me, to rip off my clothes and fuck me against the nearest available surface. I didn't expect him to recreate one of the dirtiest near misses we've had over the last two years.

"Wet," Shane murmurs. "Were you that wet for me that day? Would you have let me…" He pushes two broad fingers into me. "You would have, wouldn't you?"

"Yes," I moan. I writhe back against his touch, trying to take him deeper. I feel like I'm on fire, wanton and dirty and unable to stop. "I wanted your fingers so bad."

Just like that, they're gone. "You want to be bad, Lily? Prove it."

I lift my head. "How?"

"Come here."

I turn around to find he's spread his legs a little and has his hand palm up on his thigh. His fingers are still wet with my desire, and that might embarrass me if I had room for thought. Shane nods at his fingers. "Straddle my thigh. Right here."

Understanding dawns, bringing with it another wave of need. I have to grip his shoulders as I obey, and I come down lightly against his palm. Shane rewards me be pushing his fingers into me again. This time, I can't help whimpering.

"Take what you need, Lily." He grips my hip with his free hand and urges me to rock against his palm. "Ride my hand."

I shiver. "Your hand isn't what I want."

"My hand is all you get right now. You have to earn my cock." He smiles, slow and arrogant. "I'm not a little prick who's desperate to fuck your pussy and chase my own pleasure. I'll get inside you when I'm good and ready, and not a moment before." His voice goes hard. "Ride my hand, Lily." He leans in, his voice low and sinful. "Show your Daddy how prettily you come."

Calling him that is downright wicked. "Okay," I breathe. And then I begin to move, grinding against his palm, forcing his fingers as deep in me as I can get them. It's not enough, but it feels so good and so bad at the same time. It's made more complicated by the fact that I'm in a familiar setting, but things couldn't be more different.

Shane watches me a moment, his gaze dark and hungry and then leans down and captures my nipple through the thin fabric of my dress. He sucks hard, making me cry out, and then looks up. "Take off the dress."

I'm only too happy to comply. I wrestle it off me and toss it away. The way he watches me—God, I can't breathe. My orgasm is bearing down on me, so I slow, wanting to make this last as long as I can. I lean back and prop my hands on the ottoman, giving him view of the long line of my body as I fuck his hand. His jaw goes tight. "You are so sexy."

"Thanks, Daddy."

He drags me closer. "I shouldn't like that so fucking much." He guides me to lie down between his spread thighs, my legs stretched wide as he drags me until I'm nearly in his lap. "But I do like it, Lily. I really, really do." He parts my pussy with questing fingers and circles my clit slowly with his thumb. "Do you want to come?"

I think I might die if I don't. "Yes."

He's still tracing me with his fingers, teasing me, examining me. "Tell me what this pretty pussy needs, baby girl. Ask me properly and I'll give it to you."

I bite my bottom lip and look down my body at him. Do I dare say it? The alternative—not getting what I want—is unacceptable. "Make me come, Daddy. Please."

The slow slide of his fingers into me feels obscene in this position. As if I'm just a plaything for him to do with as he pleases. Against my better judgement, my gaze flies around the room. We're totally exposed here. If someone walked in, there would be no doubt what we're doing, no hiding how close I am to coming, no missing the fact that it's *his* fingers getting me there.

"What are you thinking about?" He asks almost idly as he pumps his fingers a little. "You just clenched around me."

"I, um…" I drag in a ragged breath. "I was thinking about how exposed we are right now."

"Not we. *You* are exposed. Spread out in only these tease of garters." He spreads my pussy with his free hand and bends down to ghost his exhale against my clit. "You're thinking about the look on his face if he found us like this."

I hadn't been, but now I can think of nothing else. Fierce satisfaction soars through me. I've endured so much pain and humiliation because of Max. I'm just enough of an asshole to want to respond in kind. "Maybe."

Another delicious exhale, the feeling almost enough to tip me over the edge. "I shouldn't ask…"

I stretch my arms over my head, writhing almost mind-lessly against his touch. "Ask me. I'll tell you whatever you want."

"When's the last time he made you come, Lily?" It sounds like it's dragged from him, rough and brutal. "When's the last time he worshiped your pretty pussy the way it was meant to be worshiped? Fingers and tongue, over and over again until you're begging for his cock."

My back bows and the beginning of an orgasm curls my toes. I'm so close... But Shane's stopped moving, stopped the heady rise of pleasure while he waits for my answer. I whine and thrash. "Never. He's never done any of that."

"He's never made you come?"

"No." He never seemed to care, either. Not as long as he got his.

Shock makes his voice harsh. "Not a single fucking time?"

"No," I whimper. "Not once."

His curse is the only warning I get before his mouth is on me. Licking and sucking and, holy shit, that feels good. I barely get a chance to enjoy it before I'm orgasming, my toes curling and my back bowing. I don't mean to grab his hair and grind my pussy against his face, milking every last bit of pleasure from his clever tongue.

I don't mean to, but I'm not sorry I do it.

Shane shifts me higher on the ottoman and shoves it forward enough that he can go to his knees between my spread thighs. I tense. Most of the time when guys have gone down on me in the past, they're in a rush, doing the bare minimum to get me ready enough to fuck me. I'm *more* than ready to fuck Shane, but he's giving my pussy slow, thorough kisses. Like he has all the time in the world. Like this isn't even about my pleasure; it's simply because he's enjoying himself.

Little by little, I relax, my mind unspooling beneath his tongue and the pressure of his fingers against my thighs, holding me open for him. "That feels good," I whisper.

He drags the flat of his tongue over my clit. "Stay the long weekend."

I lift my head. "What?"

He's watching me closely. "Stay the weekend, baby girl. Let me work out two years' frustration on your tight little body and worship your pussy. Let me make you come so

13

many times, you lose count." Another long lick. "Surely that'll satisfy your need for revenge."

I can't think with him working me like this. "But what if he comes to visit?"

"He won't." He nips my thigh. "I'll tell him to stay away if that's what you want."

I don't know what I want. If this is only revenge, having Max catch us should be the ultimate goal. But if he catches us, this ends. I slowly reach down and sift my fingers through Shane's silvering hair. I lift my hips, drawing his mouth back to my pussy. "Yes, Daddy. I'll stay the long weekend."

His answering grin makes me shiver. "Good." And then his mouth is on me again, resuming his slow tongue fucking.

Even as I tell myself there's no possible way I could come again, he coaxes my pleasure higher, easing me back to that cutting edge of desire. Quicker than I imagine possible, I'm whimpering and writhing and rolling my hips to grind against his mouth. "Oh my god, why does that feel so freaking good?"

"Because." He circles my clit with the tip of his tongue. "I have nothing but time, baby girl. Nothing but time and your pussy and a whole fuck-ton of patience. You think I haven't imagined your taste? I finally get it and you think I'm going to rush? No. Fuck no."

I feel like I'm about to burst out of my skin. "Don't stop."

He doesn't answer with words, but he answers all the same. Each stroke drives me higher, winds me tighter. And then I'm at the precipice, suspended between one lick and the next, only to freefall down the other side. I come so hard, I shriek and clamp my thighs around his head. Shane wedges his big hands around them to force my legs wide again, to hold me open as he continues his assault until my bones turn to putty and I collapse. "No more. Oh god, no more."

His dark chuckle promises no mercy. "Lily, you didn't come here for two measly orgasms." He's at my pussy again, dragging his thumbs over my lips and parting me as if he can't get enough of the sight of me. "So fucking pretty and pink and wet just for me."

"Yes," the word comes out as a rasp.

Shane sits back a little but doesn't stop touching me. He avoids my clit for now, but the slow, possessive strokes against the rest of me is both easing me down and riling me back up. He doesn't take his attention from my pussy. "I'd like to remember this."

"Me too."

"No, I don't mean like that." He finally drags his gaze up to my face. My wetness is all over his mouth and chin. He looks like a fucking savage, and I love that he doesn't care that I'm all over him. We've made a mess of each other and, as he said, we're just getting started. "I want to film you, baby girl. Something just for us."

I go still. Fucking Shane is one thing. Pictures? Videos? Those are forever, no matter if they get deleted or not. There are always backups upon backups. My body shakes, and I can't decide if it's need or concern. "What will you do with it?"

"Remember the weekend when your pussy was mine and mine alone." He cups me between my thighs hard. Like he's owning that part of me, all of me. "If it makes you feel better, you can put it on your phone. Decide later if you want to send it to me or not."

It's wrong. The woman I was four days ago never would have consented to something like this, let alone actually desired it. I'm already nodding. "Yes."

15

CHAPTER 3

"*D*on't move." Shane rises to his feet and stalks out of the room. I don't have time to wonder if this is all one terrible mistake before he's back, my purse in his hands. He tosses it next to me. "Phone."

I dig it out with shaking hands, unlock it, and pass it over. Shane considers me and then jerks his chin to the couch. "Sit in the corner."

I obey, moving awkwardly. I lean back against the corner of the couch and spread my legs before he can command me to do it. His tight smile is reward enough. "Good girl." He stands again and flips on the lights in the living room and turns off the TV. Somehow I feel even more exposed than I have so far tonight as Shane kneels back between my thighs and lifts my phone. "The trees will keep the neighbors from getting nosy."

"Too bad," I murmur. I reach up and back to grip the couch. "I think they'd like the show."

"No doubt." He pushes the button to start the camera, panning it across my lower body. "Needy pussy. Look how wet and plump you are." Shane drags two fingers down my slit, parting me obscenely. "So fucking needy. You want my cock, but you don't get it yet, do you? You haven't *earned* it yet." He pushes a single finger into me and then joins it with a second. "You going to take my cock just as eagerly as you take my fingers?"

"Yes, Daddy," I whisper. I watch him slowly slide his fingers in and out of me until they're coated with my wetness, until they shine in the camera on my phone.

"That's right. Watch your Daddy fuck you with his fingers like the dirty little slut you are." He hardly sounds like himself, his voice going rough and edged. "I think you can take another one." He wedges a third finger into me. It's almost too much, and I can't stop the whimper that escapes my lips.

Shane gives me a sharp look. "You take what I give you. Do you hear me? You take my three fingers, and you say thank you when I make you come again."

Panic and desire wind through me. I want what he's telling me, but I can't possibly. "I can't."

"What the fuck did you just say?" He drives his fingers into me hard, bowing my back, but before I can adjust, he withdraws and grabs my chin the same way he did in the kitchen, shoving two fingers deep. I'm vaguely aware of the phone pointed at my face, but my attention is consumed by him, by the brutal look on his face. He fucks my mouth with his fingers, forcing me to taste myself there, forcing me to acknowledge that I'm just as much a dirty little slut as I'm pretending to be.

That maybe I'm not pretending at all.

I gag hard, and only then does he slide his fingers out of my mouth, slowly, reminding me who's in charge with both his pace and his remaining grip on my chin. "What did you say to me?" he repeats softly.

There are tears on my face, but I feel like I'm on fire as I stare at him. I slowly lick my lips. "Yes, Daddy." My voice is hoarse. It's strange to talk around his grasp digging into my chin. "I'll take your fingers and thank you when you make me come again."

Shane's gaze drops to my lips and then he drags me to his mouth.

I have spent far longer than I'll ever admit wondering what it would be like to be kissed by this man. Fantasy doesn't come close to reality. There's no tentativeness, certainly no gentleness. He takes my mouth like a conquering king, forcing me wide to allow his tongue, angling me exactly where he wants me. He fucking *plunders* me. Somehow the kiss is just as erotic as everything we've done so far, only made more so that I can taste evidence of myself all over his tongue. I'm *all over him.*

I forget about the camera. I forget about everything except my need for him. I drag my mouth from his and sob against his lips. "Please fuck me. I need you."

Shane exhales harshly against my mouth. "There are condoms in the bathroom cabinet. Go get them."

I don't question his order. I simply obey, climbing to my feet and hurrying into the small downstairs bathroom to get a string of condoms. When I get back to the living room, he's on the couch and pulling his cock out. I stop short. Holy shit, he's huge. Like really, really huge. "Whoa."

Shane gives me his arrogant grin. "Get over here and get on your Daddy's cock like a good little girl."

He grabs the condoms from me and rips one open, rolling it over his length as I watch. I can't catch my breath, can't do anything but move to straddle him and shiver as he notches his cock at my entrance. I half expect him to drive up into me, but Shane sits back and lets me make this choice. As if I had any other destination in mind when I showed up here tonight. Somehow, through all the hazy reasoning that put me on this path, I never expected to enjoy myself so much.

I let gravity make the choice for me, sinking slowly onto his length. Except that only goes so far. He's too big to slide in with a single stroke the first time, and I'm left panting and writhing and trying to take him deeper. "God, that feels good."

"Take it all." His hands on my hips, slowly, inexorably dragging me down until I'm sure I can feel him in the back of my throat. "There you go." He sounds almost kind, almost caring, as he impales me on his cock. Shane hooks the back of my neck and then his mouth is on mine again, kissing me like he needs me more than air to breathe.

I fight my way up his cock and then resume my journey, fucking him slowly until my body accommodates, and then moving faster. The rest of the scene registers in between slow blinks. The fact that he's still fully clothed. How naked I am by comparison. It's like a continuation of our power dynamic, but I can't tell if I'm the tempting siren or the submissive. I don't know which I want to be.

"You've wanted this cock a long time, haven't you?" His voice rips me out of my daze. "Walking around my house in those little teases of outfits, bending over a little too far so I almost see your pretty pussy. You wanted to tempt me."

"Maybe," I whisper. "I liked the way you looked at me. I liked thinking about being bad with you." I never would have done it if things didn't come to this point... At least, I don't think I would have. But that doesn't stop us from spinning out our unforgivable fantasy. I brace my hands on his shoulders and grind down hard on his cock. "I didn't have to walk in a towel from the bathroom to his room. I didn't have to slow down every time I walked past your bedroom like that."

"I know." He tightens his grip on my hips, urging me to move faster.

"I almost dropped the towel once." I don't even know if it's the truth. I don't care. "Just to see how you'd react." I can almost picture it, my new version of the events that day, of catching sight of him in his bedroom, watching me with those dark eyes, pinning me in place. Of letting the towel fall... "What would you have done?"

"Told you to come into my bedroom and shut the door." He yanks me down on his cock, holding himself deep inside me. "Don't lock it, though. Because that's what you want, isn't it? To be dirty and to be bad and to fuck me when you shouldn't."

"I'm not the only one who wants to be dirty and bad, am I?" I lean down and lick the shell of his ear. "I'm not the one fucking my son's ex-fiancé right now, am I? I'm not the one who stood a little too close, who watched me a little too intensely, who licked his lips every time my skirt slid a little too high."

"Yeah, well, it's my cock you're riding right now. Not his." He hooks me around the waist and tumbles me back onto the couch. That's when I see my phone, carefully positioned to catch the perfect shot to see his cock slide into me. It's an even better angle now, my body splayed out as he holds himself up and drives into me. Putting on a show for the camera. I can perfectly see my breasts shake with the force of every thrust, can see his cock, slick with my desire, disappearing into me, spreading my pussy with his width. "Who's cock do you need, baby girl?" he grinds out. "Say it."

I meet my own gaze in the camera. I have never, ever done anything like this before. Apparently this weekend will be one of firsts. I intentionally look away from my phone, look up to find him staring down at me as if he wants to draw forth every filthy fantasy from my head. I hold his gaze as I say, "Your cock, Daddy. I need your cock."

CHAPTER 4

"*T*hat's right." Shane shoves into me hard enough that it drives me several inches up the couch. "My cock."

He fucks me like he's mad at me. Like by showing up here tonight I've opened Pandora's box for both of us and now we can never shut it again. It's fierce and just shy of brutal, like he wants to punish me for making him want me.

I love every second of it.

This time, my orgasm has teeth and claws and rips me to pieces as I come. I twist and bite his arm, needing some kind of outlet for the pleasure that's bordering on pain. Shane curses and digs his hand into my hair, prying me off him. His strokes become rougher, more frenzied and he buries his face in my neck as he comes.

I stare up at the ceiling as our harsh breathing becomes the only sound in the room. Part of me can't believe what we just did. The rest of me is wondering when we can do it again. He asked me to stay the weekend, but surely that's not what he actually wants? He's assuaged his curiosity now, slaked his lust. He'll get me dressed and send me on my way now. Surely.

I'm so busy preparing myself for that swift exit that it takes me several long second to register that he's leveraged himself up and is searching my face. "Lily." There's a note of concern in the way he says my name, as if it's not the first time.

"What?"

"Did I hurt you?" He slides his hand along the base of my skull where my scalp is smarting a little from how roughly he yanked me off him. It's barely a twinge, but I have to fight down the impulse to rub all of me against all of him at the careful way he touches me now, when a few short minutes ago he was manhandling me while spilling filth into my ears. The contrast should be jarring, but it just feels sexy as hell. "Lily, answer me."

"I'm fine." My voice is raspy. "Better than fine." I clear my throat. "Sorry about your arm."

"It's nothing." He clasps my chin, so much gentler than the last time and studies my face. "You'd tell me if I hurt you." It doesn't come out like a question. It comes out like a command.

I lick my lips. "Yes, I'd tell you."

Whatever he sees in my expression seems to be enough for him because he nods and moves off me. Out of me. I whimper a little at the loss and shove the sound down deep. I don't want him to misunderstand it.

Shane looks down at his cock and grimaces. "Give me a second."

"Sure." I manage to drag myself into a seated position by the time he returns from the bathroom, his clothing righted. He looks at me for so long, I brace myself. This is where he ushers me out.

Finally Shane shakes his head. "You still want that drink?"

I blink. "Um. Yes?"

"Lose the garters and tights." He doesn't wait for a response. He just walks away, expecting me to obey.

And I do. I unclasp the garters and peel off the tights, and then slip off the belt itself. When he returns a few minutes later with fresh drinks, I'm standing there naked, not sure what to do. We just fucked on the couch, but it feels weird as hell to just sit down.

Shane stops when he sees me and arches his brows. "Problem?"

I lift my hands and then let them drop. "In my head, this ended when we both orgasmed. I don't know how to handle this." I motion between us.

If anything, his brows rise higher. "Lily," he says my name slowly. "You called me Daddy while you came on my cock, and *this* is what makes you feel awkward?"

Heat surges beneath my skin, and I don't have to look down to know I'm blushing. "It's different."

"No shit." He walks slowly toward me and passes over my drink. I raise it and take a long sip. It's cool and fruity and exactly how I like it. Shane drops onto the couch and crooks his fingers at me. "Come here."

I expect—But then, I should know better by now. If I had a plan coming into tonight, we've gone off the rails. Apparently we're going to *keep* going off the rails. I let Shane pull me down into his lap and even though we've now had sex, I can't quite get over how much bigger he is than I am. His son is built leaner, but Shane is all broad warrior. Age hasn't softened him a single bit. He runs his callused hands up my outer thigh to my hip. "I'm sorry."

"You didn't do anything I didn't come here for."

He makes a face. "Not about that. Not about what I'm going to do to you the second I'm recovered." He gives my hip a light squeeze as if he can't help touching me, as if he's

23

not quite sure this is real. "I'm sorry that he was so fucking stupid to throw someone as special as you away."

"Shane." I wait for him to look at me. "I really, really don't want to talk about it."

"Too bad, baby girl. You came here looking for revenge, and if I'm going to take part in that, then you're going to have to bend, too." He skates his hand back down to my knee, a slow drag that might be comfort or might be the beginnings of a new seduction. "I thought I raised him better, but I fucked up somewhere along the way."

I'm not in the mood to defend either Shane or Max. It doesn't fucking matter that Max isn't a total piece of shit, even if he is a cheating asshole. Maybe the relationship felt just as off to him as it did to me and that was his only way of dealing with it. It doesn't excuse what he did—nothing can do that—but surely I wouldn't have been touching myself to thoughts of his dad if things were perfect in our relationship. I take another swallow of my drink. "It wasn't right between us. I think we both wanted it to be, but it wasn't."

He mirrors my thoughts with his words. "That doesn't excuse what he did."

"No, it doesn't." Slowly, oh so slowly, I lay my head on his shoulder. "I'm probably a right asshole to be here right now."

"Let's just say there's enough asshole in this situation to go round." He sighs. "Too late to take it back now."

Against all reason, that makes me smile. I twist to look up at him. "You mean you don't want to go back to an hour ago before you knew what my pussy tastes like?"

He taps a stern finger against my lips, but his dark eyes twinkle. "You've got a mouth on you, baby girl."

I lean forward and catch his finger between my teeth and then suck it into my mouth. I don't know what I'm doing. Maybe I'm tired of talking about Max and realizing that I'm just as bad as he is right now, or maybe I just can't stand the thought of being this close to Shane without having some part of him inside me. The reason doesn't matter. His reaction does.

He twists his wrist and grasps my chin, his eyes going hard in a way that makes my body sing to life. "I would have thought you'd need more time to recover after what we just did."

I would have thought so, too, but I'm already fighting not to squirm in his lap. I swirl my tongue around his finger and beg him with my eyes. I don't even know what I'm begging for. It doesn't matter. Shane seems to know.

He takes my glass from my hand, sets it on the side table next to his, and then shifts me around until my back is against his chest. I'm still trying to figure out where this is going, to anticipate his next touch, when he starts idly running his hands up and down my body. My hips. My sides. Palming my breasts. Up to bracket my throat and then moving back down. "Needy little slut," he murmurs in my ear. "You get a taste for orgasms at my hand and that's all you want, isn't it?"

I shamelessly spread my legs, trying to will him to touch me. "Yes. That's what I want."

"Thought you said you couldn't go again." His rough hand comes down on my pussy, clenching me almost tightly enough to hurt. I've never felt so fucking owned in my entire life. He grips me like I'm his, and I'm suddenly not sure he's wrong.

My breath saws in my lungs. Did he ask a question? I don't know and I can't think to ask. For his part, Shane keeps gripping me tightly as he drags his mouth over my shoulder and up to my neck. "You're always playing the tease, baby girl. Teasing me for two long years, and then you finally gift me with this pussy and tease me like you're only going to give me three bullshit orgasms. This pussy?" He slaps me hard enough to make me flinch back against him. "It's mine for the next three days."

"But—" I don't even know why I'm arguing. This is what I want.

"No." He gives my pussy another slap. "Who's this pussy belong to for the next three days?"

Against all reason, my throat gets tight. I blink rapidly. "You."

Another slap. "Do better."

I swallow hard, my voice thick. "It's your pussy, Daddy."

"That's right." Just like that, his touch turns soft and almost tender, dragging his fingers over my slit. "It's my pussy. And I say when you've had enough. We're not done tonight, are we?"

I lean my head back against his shoulder as a tear slips free. I spread my legs wider yet. "No, Daddy. We're not done tonight."

CHAPTER 5

"Good girl." Shane reaches over and grabs the throw, pulling it over us and covering me from the neck down. I tense, but he just picks up the remote and puts the movie back on, restarting it.

I frown at the television. "I thought you said we weren't done."

"We aren't. Sit back and relax." He bands an arm around my waist, urging me to lean more comfortably against his chest.

I try. I really do. But he's so hard at my back and I'm surrounded by him, his big arms holding me to him, his mouth tracing lazy patterns on the side of my neck, his hand...

He barely lets it get through the opening credits before he's palming my pussy again. "How many times did we watch movies over the last two years?"

I hold perfectly still, my legs quivering from the effort. "Not like this."

"No, not like this." He traces a blunt finger around my opening. "You'd have to be feeling particularly brave to sit down here in nothing more than a throw blanket and watch a movie and expect me not to do anything about it."

"Mmm." I hiss out a breath as he circles my clit. "You'd have to think of a good reason to get me on your lap to take advantage of it."

"I'd trip you." He laughs roughly in my ear. "Clumsy girl, landing right where I want you. I'd try to help you get on your feet, of course, but then I touch this pussy and it's all over."

"Or... Maybe you wouldn't have to play games, Shane." I finally move, running my hands down his arms until my hand is over his where he's touching me. "Maybe I'd take your hand and guide it right where I'm aching for you."

He nips my earlobe. "Dirty girl. So fucking *needy.*"

"No one has to know. Except...oops." I shrug and the blanket slips off my shoulders to pool at my waist. "Better hope no one walks in."

"It's like you want to be caught." He pushes two fingers into me slowly, agonizingly slowly, and withdraws. "Like you want someone to walk in and know I've got my fingers in your pussy."

I look down. It's easy enough to see the movement of his hand under the thin fabric. "They'd know."

"Yes, baby girl, they'd know." His dark chuckle makes me writhe. "Would you like to go for a drive tomorrow? Right in the afternoon while traffic is at its worst. I'll slip my hand up your skirt and we'll count how many people notice."

"Oh *fuck.*"

He keeps up his slow finger fucking. "You want that?"

"Yes, Daddy. I want that." I watch the movement of the blanket, somehow just as hot as actually watching his fingers penetrate me.

"Lily." The rough tone of his voice lashes. "If you can

manage to stay still through this movie, I'll take you upstairs and fuck you properly."

"What we did on the couch wasn't a proper fucking?"

Another of those dark chuckles. "Not even close. That was just to take the edge off."

Time ceases to have any meaning as he slowly plays with my pussy while the movie runs in the background. I stare at the moving images, but my entire being is focused on the slow slide of Shane's fingers, on the way he brands me with his touch. I have the half-hysterical thought that this was a terrible mistake. How can any sex compare to this? Am I peaking at twenty-six, destined to spend the rest of my life mourning the fact that I'll never meet another man who commands my pleasure the way this one does?

Shane doesn't let me come. Not once. He brings me to the edge over and over again, easing me away from it every single time. By the time the credits roll, I'm shaking so hard, he has to pin me to his lap to keep me in place. He circles my clit slowly until the last name scrolls past and the movie returns to the menu. "Good girl."

"Fuck you," I grit out.

"Want me to kiss it and make it better?"

I almost tell him to fuck off. I'm so poised on the edge, a gentle breeze might tip me over. But I want his mouth too bad to cut off my nose to spite my face. "Yes."

"Yes…"

My face flames, but I'm too far gone to care. "Lick my pussy, Daddy. Make me come all over your face."

He exhales harshly. "Dirty, dirty girl. You want me to do all the work, is that it?"

"What?"

Shane's already moving, shifting me off his lap, grabbing a pillow, and laying down on the ottoman with his head toward the windows lining the wall that look into the backyard. He arches an eyebrow. "You want my tongue in your cunt? Get over here and ride my face."

I scramble to obey, moving to his chest and then gasping as he lifts me up to straddle his face. With the pillow beneath his head, the angle is perfect. But he doesn't immediately release me. "Look up."

I obey and gasp. The windows act as mirrors, reflecting the image of us. All I can see are his massive hands at my hips and the salt and pepper of his head between my thighs. And me. I can see *all* of me. Narrow waist, flushed breasts, my hair tangled in a way that can only be caused by fucking. I look devious.

"You like the way you look with your Daddy's head between your thighs?"

"Yes," I whisper. I look down at him. "I like the sight of your mouth on my pussy even more. In fact..." I move off him long enough to grab my phone. I feel reckless and invincible as I perch on his upper chest. I lift my phone and press the button. "Lick my pussy, Daddy. Please."

He stares straight into the camera as he parts my pussy with this thumbs and drags his tongue over me. I stop the video and take a picture instead. It is *so* filthy. The fact that he's got his mouth on such an intimate part of me, yes, but also the look in his eyes. Like this is just the beginning and he's going to do every single depraved thing he's ever wanted to do to me.

Shane grabs the phone and tosses it onto the couch. I glare. "Hey!"

"There go you again, expecting me to do all the work." He gives my thigh a slap. "Ride my mouth, Lily. Ride it hard and dirty and I'll let you have my cock again."

I've been on the edge too long. I barely get to enjoy this moment before I'm coming. I grind down on his mouth and Shane meets me halfway, shoving his tongue inside me like he wants to lick up every bit of my orgasm. I slump down, and this time, there is no tenderness for me. He scoops me up and marches up the stairs to his bedroom. He doesn't even bother to shut the door before he has me on the bed, his mouth on mine.

I shove at his shirt. "You're wearing too many clothes."

"Lie still and spread your legs."

I immediately obey. I've seen Shane without his shirt, of course. He spent nearly as much time in his pool the last two summers as I have. He's honestly got a better body than Max does. Shane *works* on his body, and the evidence is there in the lines of muscle on display. Then he takes off his pants and I forget to breathe. I've had his cock inside me, but somehow seeing it without all the clothing to distract me makes it seem even larger.

He crawls back onto the bed and settles between my thighs, giving me one long drugging kiss. I start to wrap my legs around his waist, but he pushes them wide again.

I stare dazedly at him, hating the distance between us, small though it is. "I need you."

"You have me." But he's got a strange sort of look on his face, dark and possessive. Shane leans back and takes his cock in his hand. We both watch as he circles the head over my clit. "That feels good doesn't it, baby girl."

"Yes," I moan. I can barely keep my eyes open. My chest is heaving, my legs shaking. There's been too much pleasure in too short a time and I'm in danger of having an out of body experience. Maybe that's why it takes me a moment to notice that he's dipped his cock down to drag through my folds. Up and down, up and down, his gaze on where the broad head of him parts me with every stroke.

I bite my bottom lip. "We shouldn't. We should get a condom." Except I sound like I'm asking him instead of telling him. Like I'm hoping he'll ignore me and pave the way for us to be oh so bad. Reckless. So fucking reckless. I don't care. It feels too good to stop.

"You're right." But he doesn't stop that slow dragging motion, circling my clit and then descending again. Except this time, his broad cock presses against my entrance. "Look at how greedy your pussy is. You're practically pulling me in."

I reach down, trailing my fingers over my sweat-slicked stomach and lower to where the head of his cock is almost, *almost* inside me. I make a V with my fingers and drag them over my pussy lips, pressing them around the head of him.

"Jesus *fuck*," he growls.

"We really, really shouldn't." But I do it again. It's not enough. It's nowhere near enough. I press my fingers to either side of his cock and lift my hips, guiding him into me the tiniest bit. "It hardly counts if it's only this, right?"

"Baby girl." The threat is back in his voice. "If you let my cock inside without a condom, that's how you get it for the next three days. I'm going to pump you so full of come it's dripping down your legs. Make sure that's what you want."

"But Daddy... You said we shouldn't." I can't quite catch my breath. I keep stroking his cock where it's disappearing into my pussy. Just the head, just the tip, just enough that I can't take it back. I roll my body, fucking that part of him while he holds perfectly still. I pull him out and urge him to circle my clit again and then guide him back down to press inside. Just a bit more this time. A fraction of an inch. And then out and up over my clit. Again and again, working him a little deeper each time. Teasing him. Tempting him.

He stops me when his cock is halfway lodged inside me. "Lily, you're trying my patience."

"Look at us," I whisper. "Look how wide you spread me, how wet you make me." I roll my hips. "Do you really want to stop?"

"No, baby girl. I don't want to stop." But he still doesn't

move, still staring at his cock in my pussy as if the sight torments him. Shane finally looks up. "You better be careful. You keep acting like the perfect little slut, and I'm liable to keep you."

He doesn't give me a chance to answer, to even comprehend his words. He simply drives his cock the rest of the way into me. Once. Twice. A third time. And then he's gone, flipping me onto my stomach like I'm a doll built for his pleasure and his pleasure alone. He yanks my hips into the air and then he's inside me again, fucking away all thoughts of *should* and *shouldn't*.

Shane's hand lands on the mattress and his right hand snakes down my stomach to press against my clit. "I should send that video to my piece of shit son. Show him how you like to be fucked. Show him what he's never going to have again."

Maybe I should feel bad about the thought of Max seeing the video of me riding his father's cock. I don't. It fills me with a fierce joy that borders on rage. Apparently Shane's feeling it, too. He slams into me harder, driving me to grind on his palm. "It's not his pussy anymore, is it?"

"No," I gasp.

"That's right. Not his pussy at all." He bites my neck. "Tell me who your pussy belongs to, Lily."

"It's your pussy, Daddy."

"And I'm fucking you bare, aren't I? My big cock stretching you wide. Your tight little cunt taking every single fucking inch." He growls against my neck. "You feel so good, baby girl. All wet and slippery and made just for me."

I should put a stop to this possessive talk. This is only for the weekend, after all. It wasn't even supposed to be that long. But I don't want to. He makes me feel fucking priceless when he's saying these things, and I'm suddenly terribly afraid that I'll never get enough.

Not of Shane's cock.

Not of Shane himself.

Instead, I slam back against him as much as I'm able. "Fill me up, Daddy." I don't even know what I'm saying, only that I want this feeling to go on forever. Wicked. Dirty. Fucking *filthy*. "Fill me up with your come."

"Dirty. Little. Slut." Each word is punctuated by a savage thrust. He grinds into me and I swear I can feel his cock jerk as he comes. He slumps to the side, taking me with him, and slides a hand down to idly caress my clit. I jerk. The feeling of him going soft inside me is strange but not unpleasant, especially when he keeps up that achingly gentle circling. "Once more. One more time and you can rest."

This time, I don't tell him it's impossible. I just stretch out against his big body and let him have his way with me. It's almost like handing over that control flips a switch inside me. Like once I stop worrying about the pressure to come, my orgasm is waiting in the wings. It lifts me up and washes me out to sea. I'm vaguely aware of words coming out of my mouth, but I've lost the ability to comprehend them. It doesn't matter. Not when he's easing me back into my body, piece by piece, until I am well and firmly tethered to the earth.

Shane slips out of me and nudges me onto my back. The look on his face... I don't know that emotion, don't know what to do with it. It's almost a relief when he kisses me and I can close my eyes and just enjoy him without thinking too hard. By the time he finally lifts his head and moves off me, I feel almost like myself again.

At least the version of myself that showed up at this house to fuck my almost-father-in-law.

CHAPTER 6

"*S*tay."

I open my eyes. "I already said I would."

Shane gives me a long look. "You've had one foot out the door the second you started coming down." He shakes his head and pulls me up. "Stop thinking so hard and enjoy this, Lily."

My knees don't feel quite solid, but I manage to keep my feet as he leads me into his bathroom. I look at my reflection in the mirror. "I'd say I'm enjoying myself." My lipstick is barely more than a memory and the smudged mascara around my eyes is a far cry from the sexy smoky eye look that I started with. Not to mention that my hair has gone from playfully messy to straight up rat's nest. My gaze tracks my naked body, taking in the whisker burn on my neck and thighs, how pink and wet my pussy looks from everything we've done.

Shane walks up behind me and, holy shit, we look good. His wide shoulders dwarf me and when he sets his big hands on my waist, I feel both breakable and protected at the same time. His hair is a mess from my fingers and he's got scratches on his shoulders and the bite mark on his forearm.

We both look like sexy messes.

He pulls me back against him and cups my pussy. Not like he's trying to start us up again. More like he's touching me because he can. "Sore?"

"A little."

He nods as if he expects nothing less. "I'd say I'll give you a break tomorrow, but it's a lie." He slowly, slowly, lifts his hand, almost as if the move pains him, and turns to the shower. "Let's get some sleep."

Somehow, with everything else going on, it never occurred to me that I'd be *sleeping* with Shane. Fucking, yes. Lying in bed next to? No way.

I get tenser and tenser as we take turns in his shower and end up back in his bedroom. Shane takes one look at my face and frowns. "Get over here."

"Actually, I—"

"Lily, did I fucking stutter?"

My heart starts hammering and I move toward him one slow step at a time. He catches my hips and pulls me against him, and then grasps my chin, lifting my face so I have nowhere to hide. "Tell me."

Beneath his firm expression, it's the truth that slips free. "It feels intimate."

He arches his brows. "I've had my hands and tongue and cock inside you and *this* feels intimate." He backs me toward the bed, and I have to climb onto the mattress to keep from being toppled. "You know why that is?"

"No?"

"Because it *is* fucking intimate. You're in my bed and you're saying you feel safe enough with me to sleep." He follows me onto the bed. "You're saying you want to wake up in the morning with my tongue in your cunt. Doesn't that sound *intimate* to you?"

I swallow hard. "I'm afraid I'm going to like it too much."

At that, his gaze goes soft and devastatingly possessive. "You will. You'll like this just like you've loved everything we've done so far." Shane releases me and yanks back the blankets. He doesn't speak again until he's settled under them, sitting with his back against the headboard. "I'm not going to force you, though. If this makes you uncomfortable, I can crash on the couch." He gives a wicked grin. "But you're still going to wake up with me tongue-fucking you."

I shiver. I almost wish he hadn't given me a choice, because this would be so much easier. A revenge fuck is one thing. Intimacy feels like it's coloring outside the lines, like I'm setting myself up for a broken heart with a broken-heart chaser.

I wish I could be colder. I wish I didn't crave the feeling of his arms around me. I wish a lot of things as I tentatively crawl beneath the covers next to Shane.

He wastes no time flipping off the light and slipping down in the bed, pulling me with him. The next thing I know, we're spooning and he's got his arms wrapped around me. The man holds me like I'm the most precious thing in the world, and despite myself, I slip into sleep with his body cradling mine.

Little things wake me. Hot open-mouthed kisses at the back of my neck. Callused hands palming my breasts. A hard cock against my ass. Shane lightly pinches my nipples. "Awake?"

"Mmm." I stretch, rolling my hips to rub my ass on his cock. "I seem to remember you promising to wake me up in a very different way."

His rough chuckle has my thighs clenching together. "Just checking in, baby girl. That still what you want?"

I twist in his arms and he lets me, shifting to give me room to sling my leg up around his waist. I wrap my fist around his cock and drag his broad head over my slit. I'm already wet from how he was touching me, already aching for him. "Does it feel like that's what I want?"

Shane digs his hand into my hair and urges my head back so he can growl in my ear. "You have a slutty little pussy. We both know that. It's your head that I'm concerned with right now." His rough words are matched by the intent look on his face. I've never had a man look at me the way Shane does, as if every single thing I say is of the utmost importance. As if he really wants to know what I want, rather than have me tell him what *he* wants to hear. "Tell me what you need, Lily."

I drag in a shuddering breath and notch him at my entrance. I'm only a little sore from yesterday, but it doesn't matter. I'm not interested in waiting. I hold his gaze. "I need my Daddy's cock."

His jaw clenches and he thrusts into me the tiniest bit. "You have a dirty mouth." He reaches up with his free hand and traces my lower lip with his thumb. "I'm going to enjoy fucking it later."

I lick his thumb. "Use me."

"I plan on it." He kisses me, rough and intense, but he doesn't thrust into me like I expect. Shane kisses me like the head of his cock isn't inside me already, like we're just making out for the sake of making out. It frazzles my nerves, but in a way that isn't entirely pleasant. It feels like he's changing the rules, and I'm not sure if I'm okay with it.

As if he can sense my confusion, Shane rolls onto his back and takes me with him. He gives me a wicked grin and then lifts his arms to rest his head in his hands. "You want your Daddy's cock?"

I clutch onto what's rapidly becoming my foundation, my familiar territory, with both hands. "Yes."

"Then take it."

Despite being turned on already, I'm nowhere near prepared enough for his size. I have to fight my body and his to take him another inch deeper. He watches me writhe and squirm with his eyebrow cocked, seeming completely unaffected by my struggle. It's really, really hot. "Problem?"

"No."

"You sure?" He shifts a little but still makes no move to help me. "Because you say you want my cock, but you're not taking it like the good girl I know you can be."

I sob out an exhale as I sink another inch onto him. Holy shit, was he this big last night? I've never had a problem doing the bare minimum of foreplay before sex, but I've also never been in an experience like this. And Shane is fucking huge. Something like humiliation heats my skin, but it gets all tangled up with need. I circle my hips, trying to force him deeper. "I'm trying."

"Mmm." He watches me for a few moments and then sighs in something like disappointment. "Lily..."

"I'm *trying*." Against all reason, my lower lip quivers. What the hell is going on? I plant my hands on his chest and sink down a little more. He's too big, I'm too full, I don't know if I'm enjoying this or if it just aches. "I'm trying, Daddy. I promise."

Another of those disappointed sighs and he finally moves, his hands falling to my hips. "Stubborn to the very end."

"What?"

"You need something from me, Lily? Fucking ask for it." He lifts me off his cock and sets me on his hard stomach. Shane holds my gaze as he wets his thumb and then presses it to my clit. A slow circle has me fighting not to roll my hips. On the third one, I forget myself and do it. I grind down on his stomach like the horny little slut I apparently am. Maybe I should be self-conscious but the way he looks at me burns me up just as much as his thumb's slow circles. "That's right, baby girl. Just like that."

Pleasure coils tighter and tighter. "Why does everything you do to me feel so good?"

"Because I know what I'm doing." He urges me up a little and pushes two fingers into me, spreading me more with each stroke. "Because we fit in a twisted sort of way. You want a Daddy to give you permission to be bad. I want a baby girl who will give me that pussy whenever I want it, however I want it." Something like conflict passes over his expression. "Not just any baby girl, Lily."

What's he saying? That I'm special? I might laugh if I could find the breath for it. If I was so special, I wouldn't be in this position to begin with. I wouldn't have already started to crave the depraved games we play. I sure as hell wouldn't get off on calling him Daddy, wouldn't have fantasized about it while I was still with his son.

"Shane..."

But he doesn't give me a chance to find the words to ruin this. He hefts me up to straddle his face and then his mouth is on my pussy and I'm not worried about anything but the orgasm barreling down upon me. Coward that I am, I let him distract me, let myself ride his face as he fucks me with his tongue.

"Oh *shit.*" I come so hard, I have to plant my hands on the headboard to keep from collapsing. And Shane doesn't stop. He holds me in place and keeps kissing my pussy like he has all the time in the world. "Fuck, fuck, *fuck.*" I bite down hard on my bottom lip. "I love what you do to me."

"Don't move." He slides down and then he's at my back, his hands on either side of mine on the headboard. Shane nudges my thighs wider and thrusts slowly into me. This time, my body welcomes him and he sinks to the hilt in one smooth stroke. He keeps us like that, him impossibly deep, his big body surrounding me, his rough breathing in my ear. "What's the problem, baby girl? You worried you like this too much? That three days won't be enough?"

That's exactly what I'm worried about. No matter how much I genuinely like Shane, no matter how much I've enjoyed my time spent with him over the last two years, no matter how hard he makes me come, this *can't* last more than the weekend. I try to thrust back onto him, but there's nowhere to go. He has me pinned with his cock and body. Even though he's covering me, even though I can't see his face, I've never felt so exposed. "I was engaged to your son four days ago. I dated him for two years."

"You were. You did." He withdraws the tiniest bit and pumps into me, drawing a moan from my lips. Shane kisses my neck, my shoulder, and then his voice is in my ear again, growling things we have no business talking about while he's balls deep inside me. "He's an idiot. Maybe he'll grow out of it. Maybe he won't. It doesn't matter, because he's not for you."

"You were going to be my father-in-law!"

He nips my earlobe. "And now I'm your Daddy. I think we both prefer it this way."

CHAPTER 7

Shane keeps fucking me with those shallow strokes that feel good, but are nowhere near enough. "Stop thinking about what you *should* want, Lily."

Easy for him to say. Or maybe it isn't. I don't care. I'm not interested in being fair right now. "What if Max tries to win me back?"

Shane laughs. The bastard *laughs*. "Try it and see what happens." He releases the headboard with one hand to snake down my stomach and press to my clit. "The first time you visit this house, you're going to look at the ottoman and think about how many times you came for me there. You're not going to be able to walk past this room without remembering how good my cock feels inside you." He drags his mouth over the back of my neck. "How long do you think you'll last before you're crossing a line, Lily? An hour? Two? I bet you'd wear a short little skirt for just the occasion and slip my hand under it the second he looks the other way."

My body goes white hot at the thought. I can't breathe past wanting to do exactly that. It scares me how much I want it. "Fuck you."

"Mmm." He gives my clit a casual slap. "Hit too close to home?"

"Why are you doing this?" I whisper.

"I meant what I said last night." He slowly drags his fingers over my clit. "You make me want to keep you."

He makes me want to be kept.

I shake my head. "It will never work."

Just like that, a flip is switched. "We'll talk about it later." Shane shifts back and digs his fingers into my hips. It's all the warning I get before he starts fucking me, dragging me down his length as he thrusts forward, until his filling me consumes every part of my awareness. He drives into me again and again, forcing every doubt and fear from my mind. There's no room for them right now. We're fucking like animals, hard and rough and battling out a silent debate that we're both determined to win.

Shane fights dirty, though.

He grabs one of my hands and presses it to my clit. "Make yourself feel good, baby girl."

I should deny the order, but I'm too greedy for my next orgasm. "Yes, Daddy." Pleasure rises in waves, edging me closer and closer to where I need to be.

Then he yanks me back on his cock, sealing us together too tightly for me to fight. Shane touches a wet thumb to my ass and I freeze. He squeezes my cheek, spreading me, and then presses his thumb past the ring of muscles. "Have you ever taken a man here, Lily?"

"No," I whisper. I can't stop shaking. I don't know if I want to try to get away or arch my back to take him deeper.

"Mmm." He pumps slowly, not going particularly deep, but branding this part of me all the same. "Would you like your Daddy's cock in your ass?"

I shiver. "I don't know."

He keeps working me, holding me in place. "Did I tell you to stop touching your clit?"

Immediately, I start up again, and the added sensation of this thumb confuses me. This isn't something I thought I was interested in, but with his big cock inside me and my fingers on my clit, his thumb doesn't feel...bad. My orgasm starts gaining speed again.

"Good girl." He murmurs, still fucking me with his thumb. "I think I *am* going to take this virgin ass. Not yet. But you're mine, aren't you, Lily? Every part of you. Mouth and pussy and ass. There for my pleasure whenever I decide to take it."

I stroke my clit faster, writhing as much as I'm able to. "Yes, Daddy." The closer I get to coming, the hotter his thumb feels. My breath sobs out and my control wavers. "Fuck me however you want. Make me your dirty little slut."

"I will, Lily. You can be damn sure I will." He starts moving again, thrusting with both cock and thumb. I want to last, want to keep riding this pleasure, but my body has other ideas. I come hard, clamping down on him, and the feeling of being penetrated on two fronts drives my orgasm to new heights.

Shane presses his free hand to my back, urging my face down to the mattress but keeping my ass in the air. It allows him deeper yet. I half-expect him to pound into me, but he slows down as if savoring the feel of me. He strokes a hand down my back to squeeze my other ass cheek, spreading me obscenely. "You feel so fucking good," he murmurs and pulls out almost all the way to pump just the head of his cock into me. "You look even better. I love watching your pussy spread to take me. And you take every inch, don't you, baby girl?"

I fist the sheets and moan. "Yes, Daddy."

"You'll give me anything I ask, won't you? Because you want to be good."

It's a fight not to slam back onto his cock, not to beg him to fuck me deep again. "*Yes.*"

"Good girl." He releases a long breath and then he's doing exactly what I need, shoving deep into me, once again fucking me like he's mad at me, like I've been bad and he's going to enact my penance with his cock. He curses and then he's pressed against my back again, shoving my legs wider yet. "You try to come back here as Max's girlfriend and I'm going to punish you, Lily. Do you hear me? I'm going to flip up your little tease of a skirt and paddle your ass, and then I'm going to fuck you until you scream about how good your Daddy's cock feels inside you, scream so loud he can hear you."

Holy shit.

I bury my face in the mattress and shriek as I come. This time, Shane follows me over the edge. He pounds into me, growling my name as he fills me up. Then he presses a devastatingly gentle kiss to the top of my spine as he shifts us onto our side.

I stare blindly at the wall, trying to process the sheer amount of pleasure against how hot his words make me. How wrong they are. I should leave it at that, shouldn't look deeper into them no matter what he says about keeping me. I'm not naive enough to think that anything said in the middle of sex can be held up to the light.

That doesn't stop me from speaking. "I'm not going back to him, even if he wanted to try to make things right. It's really over." When Shane doesn't respond, except to gather me closer, I find myself continuing. "Even before this, things were off. It was too...comfortable, I guess? Like friends who occasionally had sex." It was so *easy* being with Max, easy enough that I was able to ignore all the things wrong with the relationship until they accumulated to a pile neither of us could ignore any longer. "I guess that's why he started looking outside the relationship for what he needs."

"That doesn't make it hurt less now that it's over."

My throat burns and I have to blink rapidly. "No, it doesn't make it hurt less." I've lost him, either way. Even if I don't want that relationship back, even if there's a strange sort of relief now that I'm free of it, I'm still losing Max as a friend, too.

Shane eases me onto my back and looks down at me. I don't know what he sees in my face. I'm not in control enough to shield myself from him, and even when I'm at the top of my game, he seems to see right through me. He smooths my hair back. "Go take a shower and get ready. We're going out."

I grab onto the distraction he offers with both hands. "Out? Are you sure that's a good idea?" We might live outside of Chicago but each suburb is like its own little small town. The chances we have of running into someone we know is high. I'm not sure I'm ready for everyone to know how I responded to my relationship with Max falling apart. I'm not sure I ever will be.

Instead of answering, Shane gets out of bed and walks into the bathroom. A few seconds later, I hear the shower running. By the time I manage to make it in there, he's finished with his shower and has a towel wrapped around his waist. Shane jerks his chin at the shower. "Take your time." Then he disappears out the door.

There is something that feels so taboo about using his shower. Even though we've been naked together, have fucked in both the living room and his bedroom, it's almost impossible to separate the Daddy from the father-in-law. Being naked in my father-in-law's shower feels wrong. Like I'm being bad, being somewhere I shouldn't be.

I relish the feeling as I shower. Is that the only reason I enjoy being with Shane so much? Because I shouldn't be?

My situation would be so much simpler if that were the case.

By the time I finish, he reappears with a small polka dot bag I instantly recognize. Max and I only spent significant time here in the summers because of the pool, but that was enough for me to leave a small stash of my stuff in Max's old room for when I needed it. I take the bag from Shane with shaking hands. It's another reminder of where I was versus where I am now. "Thanks."

"Clothes are on the bed." He turns and walks away.

I blink. I didn't exactly expect him to ravish me the second I got out of the shower, but there's no denying a certain disappointment that he's not letting me play out my towel-dropping fantasy. It's an effort not to march after him and force his hand, but curiosity gets the better of me. Where does he want us to go? Surely it's not just a simple errand, not when we're engaging in this weekend of sheer perversity. At least, I hope not.

I take my time getting ready, just like I took my time in the shower. Part of it is perversity—wondering how long his patience will hold—and the other part is that I genuinely want to look good for him. I blow out my long blond hair and give it a toss to maximize its natural waves, and I put on a full face of makeup. It's my summer stuff, so a bronzy natural look with pretty pink lips. I smile at myself in the mirror. He said he wants to fuck my mouth later. Red would be better, but pink will do.

Once I'm ready, I head out into the bedroom and stop short. I was so distracted, I hadn't really thought about what clothes he would have for me, but Shane's laid out one of my summer outfits. It's a tiny blue and white striped skirt with a flirty flounce, white lace panties, and a white crop top.

I'm going to freeze to death.

I glare at the closed bedroom door and finally pull on the clothes. Another check in the mirror has me pressing my lips together. This outfit is one I wear over swimsuits to make them barely public appropriate. It's not meant for anything other than that. The skirt is so short that it brushes the lower curve of my ass and the crop top is an oversized boxy fit that leaves my entire stomach bare and will expose half my breasts if I lift my arms over my head. I do it anyway and relish the heat that bolts through me at the sight of my nipples peeking out.

I find Shane in the kitchen eating pancakes. He barely looks at me as he slides a second plate across the counter and sets a coffee next to it—heavy in cream and sugar, just like I prefer. "Eat."

I wait, but he seems intent on his task. Perverse irritation flares. I took my time making myself look good for him and I want acknowledgement. I clasp my hands in front of me and pour sugar into my tone. "You're not going to tell me if you like my outfit, Daddy?"

He goes still. "It's fine."

I'm still not satisfied. I feign a yawn and stretch my arms over my head, the cool air of the room teasing my exposed breasts. When I lower my arms, Shane is finally giving me his full attention. "You're dressed like a slut, Lily. You leave the house looking like that and you're not going to like what happens."

Desire thrills through my blood. "You don't like it?" I turn around and lean against the counter, feeling my skirt ride up.

"Lily." I don't hear him move, but suddenly his hands are on my hips, dragging up my skirt. "Where the fuck are your panties?"

I have to fight back a grin. *Finally* I've got the reaction I've been craving. I try to sound as innocent as possible. "I didn't want to wear them. I don't like them."

Shane squeezes my ass cheeks. His hands are so big, he only has to shift slightly for his thumbs to brush my pussy. He parts me slowly. "Who are you planning on fucking in this slutty outfit, baby girl? Because you didn't put it on solely to run errands with me."

I try to turn around, but he easily holds me in place. He's squeezing me and stroking me, but he's not giving me the contact I need. I try to roll my hips, but he's gripping me too tightly. "I'm planning on fucking you, Daddy." Frustration bubbles up, or maybe it's just that I want to push him the same way he insists on pushing me. Regardless of the reason, my mouth gets away from me. "But if you won't give me what I need, maybe I'll go find it somewhere else."

I register the absence of his touch a bare moment before he spanks me hard enough to drive a cry from my lips. "What the *fuck?*"

"That's right, Lily." He spanks me again, this time on the other cheek. "What the fuck?" A third spank has me trying to get away, but he grabs the back of my neck and holds me in place. "You want to provoke a reaction by being a little slut? This is the one you get."

A fourth strike has tears pricking my eyes and my ass feeling like it's on fire. It hurts. It hurts so fucking much, I can barely breathe, but the heat creates a pulsing in my pussy in time with my racing heart. "I'm sorry, Daddy!"

"Sorry I called you on it, more like." He doesn't spank me again. Just keeps my face pinned to the counter as he goes back to squeezing first one cheek and then the other, ramping up the heat I'm experiencing. "For that, you don't get to leave the truck."

"W-what?"

He dips his hands between my thighs and gives a derisive laugh. "You love even this. You're fucking shameless."

"I'm sorry! I won't do it again. I promise."

"Lies." Shane urges my legs wider. "But I'll give you a chance to prove it's the truth." He drags a finger through my wetness and lowers his voice. "Be a good girl. Stand exactly like this and don't move. Look out the window."

"Okay," I whisper.

His hand comes off my neck and skates down my back as he moves behind me. I hear him go to his knees and then his mouth is on my smarting ass, kissing it better. And then he spreads me and his mouth is on my pussy and up on my ass and then back down again.

I thought the front of the house was completely shielded by trees. I was wrong. I can clearly see one neighbor shoveling snow and another walking their dog. They're going about their normal lives, having no idea that Shane is on his knees behind me just out of sight, eating my ass and pussy. My legs start to tremble. "I'm not the only one who likes being bad, am I, Daddy?" He sucks hard on my clit, which is answer enough. "You love being the guy that everyone respects, the pillar of your community, the man everyone goes to when they have something they need fixed." I gasp as his tongue swirls my ass, but force the next words out. "They'd die to know that you have your mouth all over your daughter-in-law's pussy."

Shane gives me a long lick. "Ex, Lily. Ex-daughter-in-law."

I grip the counter and try to stay still. "But you wanted to do this before that was true. You wanted me to come all over your face when I was still his."

He leans back and delivers another stinging slap to my ass. "You're not his."

"No, I'm not." I watch the snow-shoveling neighbor strike up a conversation with the dog walker directly across the street. My shirt has ridden up around my shoulders, and my skirt covers absolutely nothing at all. I'm not sure if they can see me as clearly as I can see them from this angle, but the thought that they might has me arching back, offering him my pussy. "I'm yours, Daddy." When he doesn't immediately resume licking me, I whimper. "Please make me come. I promise I'll be quiet. They won't know what filthy things you're doing to me. No one will know but us."

Shane exhales against my aching flesh. "No."

I blink. "What?"

"No." He climbs to his feet and flips my skirt down. "A punishment is only a punishment if you don't enjoy it. Go get your panties on, Lily. Don't make me ask you again."

CHAPTER 8

$\mathcal{I}$ stand in a daze and stumble upstairs to obey. My whole body feels like an exposed nerve, denied pleasure even more painful than my still-stinging ass. It only gets worse when I pull the panties on. The fabric against my aching pussy and ass is agonizing.

Back in the kitchen, Shane watches me with a dangerous expression on his face while I dutifully eat my now-cold pancakes and drink my lukewarm coffee. Once he's satisfied, he leads me to the mud room and pulls one of his coats around me. It swallows me, making me feel ridiculous in my tiny skirt that barely reaches past the edge of the coat. "I'm going to freeze," I murmur.

"No, you won't." He zips it up and nudges me down to slip my heels on. I hold my breath while he's kneeling in front of me, half hoping that if I spread my legs a little more, he'll finish what he started in the kitchen.

He doesn't.

Instead, he motions me to precede him into the garage. It's open and the truck is running, so I only get a blast of freezing air to my bare legs before I haul myself up into the warm cab of the truck. Despite being a work truck, the bench seat and interior are spotless. But then, Shane holds a manager position. For all that he's technically in construction, the man wears a suit to work most days. Of course his truck looks shiny and new inside.

I'm still processing when he climbs in through the driver's door and shuts it. Shane gives me a long look. "You're not a dirty little secret."

I blink. "I might want to be a dirty little secret."

"No." He shakes his head and hauls me to the middle of the bench seat. I fight down a shiver as he buckles the seatbelt over my hips and then reaches beneath my skirt to drag his knuckles over my clit through my panties. He keeps his hand up my skirt and rubbing my pussy as he puts the truck in reverse and backs out.

Shane waves to the neighbors still out talking, the same ones I watched while he ate me out, and they wave back. They have no idea that he's dipping a finger into me at that exact moment. "Oh god." I whimper.

"Shhh. Lot of neighborhood to get through." He idly pumps his single finger as he drives, waving to every single neighbor outside as he slowly fucks me with his big finger. I'm quivering and shaking by the time we make it out of the subdivision.

And that's when the bastard removes his finger, pulls my panties back into place, and sucks his finger clean. I stare at him. "You are such an asshole."

"Punishment," he says simply.

I'm in such agony, I barely register where we're going until Shane pulls to a stop in front of a nondescript white building. The parking lot is all but empty on a Saturday morning, and the other two buildings that share the space are abandoned. I frown out the windshield. "This is a sex toy shop."

He turns to face me, suddenly taking up too much space. "I'm going to be in there for about ten minutes. During that time, I want you to bring yourself almost to orgasm, but don't go over the edge."

I lick my lips. "What happens if I do?"

"Then you don't get my cock for the rest of the day." He leans down, sexy and menacing. "You get my mouth and you get my fingers, but I'm not going to let you come. You've been denied once. Think hard about whether it's worth a full twenty-four hours of that agony."

I glare. "Asshole."

He takes my hand and shoves it down my panties. "Be a good girl and I'll give you a present when I get back."

Despite my best attempt to be irritated, I can't help perking up. "A present?"

"Yes, Lily." He chuckles and climbs out of the truck, letting in a cold blast of wind. "Lock the doors."

It's such a *dad* thing to say that I almost come on the spot.

I reach over with the hand not in my panties and lock the doors. He nods and heads into the building. I watch him go and start stroking my clit. It feels good; doing it in the middle of the day in a parking lot feels even better. I pull down the zipper of Shane's coat and part it just enough to reach in and pull my top up. Even if there was anyone around, they wouldn't be able to see anything, but knowing my breasts are bared makes me hotter.

I watch the clock, nudging myself closer and closer to orgasm. At ten minutes, Shane isn't back yet. I lean my head against the window, mindlessly rubbing on my clit. I'm *so close*. Would he really know if I came? Am I willing to risk it?

A knock on the window startles a scream out of me. I jerk upright and find Shane watching me with a disapproving look on his face. I reach over with a shaking hand and unlock the doors. He wastes no time climbing in and shutting the door. A small bag goes onto the seat on the other side of me and a second one goes on the floorboard. I don't get a chance to ask what's in either before he drives to the other side of the parking lot near a fence that borders a residential street. There are now two buildings' worth of parking lot between us and the sex shop, and I look at him in question.

He unbuckles me. "Get on your hands and knees facing the passenger door."

My eyes go wide, but I'm already scrambling to obey. He pushes up my skirt and drags my panties down a few inches. Somehow, this feels a thousand times more vulgar than when I had no panties on. He touches my pussy as if examining it. "Were you a good girl, Lily? Your pussy is awfully wet right now."

"I didn't come. I swear it."

He keeps fondling me as if he can divine the very answer out of my flesh. I watch a car pull up and park at the sex toy shop. "We're out in the open."

He ignores me. "Get in the bag and hand me the two things you find."

I have to go down onto my elbows to obey, and my shirt slides up to bunch around my upper chest. The coat still shields me, but I dig into the bag and come up with a bottle of lube and a shiny metal plug. "Shane—"

"Hand them to me."

I awkwardly obey. I listen to him open the bottle and then cool lube touches my ass and an even cooler metal presses there. "Relax," he murmurs. With one hand he keeps stroking my pussy and the other he wedges the plug into my ass. It's significantly larger than his thumb, but it doesn't hurt. It just feels like *a lot*. I am painfully aware, however, that it's nowhere near the size of his cock.

Once it's lodged inside me, he sits back and gives a sound suspiciously like a growl. "Fuck, that's pretty."

"*Shane*," I moan.

"That's even prettier." He pushes two fingers into me. The intrusion feels so much more filling with the plug in. "Say my name again, Lily."

I thrust back against his hand, shamelessly fucking his fingers. "Shane. Oh god, that feels so good."

"Mmm. You like that plug in your virgin ass." He withdraws his hand long enough to flip me onto my back and push me down onto the seat. Shane yanks my panties off and shoves up my skirt again, impaling me with his fingers. "Open the jacket and lift your top baby girl. You know you want to show me everything."

I reach down with trembling hands and pull up my crop top to expose my breasts. He palms one roughly and then the other, his expression intense as he keeps fucking me with his fingers. "You're so sexy, Lily. You're enough to make me forget myself and fuck you right here when everyone can see." He circles my clit just shy of savagely. "Do you like knowing you undo me? That I'll put it all on the line just to sink into your tight pussy?"

I moan and arch my back, trying to take him deeper, only to earn a slap on my clit. My eyes fly open to find him glaring at me. "I asked you a fucking question."

I leverage myself up onto my elbows. When he doesn't stop me, I keep going, rising onto my knees and moving to straddle him, his fingers wedged inside me all the while. I loop my arms around his neck and press myself to him, my lips at his ear. "I like it," I whisper, undulating on his fingers. "Do you know what I'd like even better?"

"Say it," he grits out.

Instead, I lean back enough to reach between us and undo his jeans. I take out his cock and stroke him. Only then does he let me nudge his hand away from me and guide him up to

YOUR DAD WILL DO

cup my breasts. Shane lets me move him around, the heat of his gaze enough to burn me to ash.

I stroke his cock again. "I want to ride your cock, Daddy." This time, my body welcomes him as I slide down his length. We both shudder when he's seated entirely inside me. He feels even bigger with the plug in my ass, and I moan and start rocking. "I want you to fill me up." I pick up my pace, nearly mindless with need. "I want your come dripping down my thighs so everyone knows who I belong to."

"*Jesus Christ.*" He pushes me back just enough to nudge the jacket wide open. If anyone were to look, there is no denying what we're doing. I'm practically naked in his lap, my hips rolling as I ride him slowly.

Shane coasts a hand up the center of my body to lightly grasp my throat. "Lily—" Movement draws his attention and he curses. While I'm still trying to process, still teetering on the edge of an orgasm, he yanks the coat back over me and zips it up. He lifts me off his cock and drops me next to him.

I look out the window and freeze. I know that car with the dent in the driver's side. That's *Max's* car.

CHAPTER 9

*B*efore I can consider what I'm doing, I throw myself flat on the seat. I look up at Shane. "Not like this. Please." Not with a plug in my ass and my thighs still wet from riding his cock. It's not even that I'm opposed to Max catching us, but I don't want it to be fucking in a parking lot like a pair of teenagers. It doesn't make sense, even to me, but Shane nods and puts the truck in gear.

He takes a right turn into traffic and his phone rings. A detached female voice on the Bluetooth tells me everything I need to know. It's Max calling. Shane answers before I can decide if I want him to or not. "What's up?"

"Were you just in the Castle parking lot? I thought I saw your truck."

Shane laughs. "It's Saturday morning. What are you and Lily up to that you're there so early?"

I stare. What a shameless bastard.

Awkward silence reigns. Finally, Max clears his throat. "We, uh, broke up earlier this week. It wasn't working out for either of us."

Shane looks down at me, his eyes sympathetic even if his

58

words are designed to split me wide open. "Moving on awful fast then, aren't you, son?"

Another awkward throat clearing. "Look, I can explain, but the short answer is that yeah, I'm seeing someone else. It's not a big deal."

It's. Not. A. Big. Deal.

Any guilt I had over what I've spent the last twenty-four hours doing goes up in smoke. I shift on the seat until I can reach the front of Shane's pants. He lets me get his cock out, but then he digs his hand into my hair and pins my head to his thigh, forcing me still. Through it all, his voice never changes. "Sounds like a big deal to me."

"Look, I know you always liked Lily, but it wasn't working out."

We stop at a light and he's watching me again, dark eyes intense. "I liked her a whole hell of a lot."

"Well then, maybe you should date her," Max snaps. "She's not for me, and if you ask her, she'd tell you that herself. I'm not here for this guilt trip. Now I've got to go. My girlfriend is waiting."

Girlfriend. Girlfriend. *Girlfriend.*

Shane hangs up and releases me in the same moment. I grab his cock and swallow him down, desperate to drive away how fucking replaceable I feel in this moment. Max wasn't just fucking his secretary. He was—is—*dating* her.

"He's an idiot," Shane say quietly.

I don't care. I'm not listening. I'm too busy fighting to take his big cock as far into my throat as I can manage. The discomfort in my jaw grounds me in a way nothing else can right now. I'm vaguely aware of us making another turn and another, of Shane finally putting the truck in park and leaning back, but it barely registers because this blowjob is the only thing that matters. If I allow myself to think of anything else, I might start screaming and never stop.

He gathers my hair in his left hand and skates his right hand down my back. He's tall enough to reach my hips easily and he starts squeezing my ass cheeks, making the plug shift inside me. "Do you hear me, Lily? I said he's a fucking idiot. He doesn't give a shit what he's throwing away. He doesn't understand what a goddamn gift you are." He presses his palm hard against the plug and shoves three fingers into me, making me moan. "You know what? I *am* going to do it. I'm going to fuck you, and I'm going to date you, and it would serve that little shit right if I married you and made you his stepmother."

I make a noise around his length, but even I don't know if it's a sound of protest or encouragement. Apparently he doesn't know either because he drags me off his cock and up to his mouth, and then *lifts* me with his fingers in my pussy to move me back onto his lap. He tightens his grip in my hair, bending me back over the steering wheel so he can drag his mouth over my breasts. "Your Daddy knows what you need, baby girl. Now get back on this cock."

I slam onto him, but it's not enough. I don't know if anything will be enough. "It hurts. It hurts so much."

"I know." Shane doesn't need me to clarify that I'm not talking about physical pain. He kisses me as I ride him, as I chase the temporary oblivion an orgasm offers. A little death, a small escape, one I need more than I need my next breath.

It hits me hard enough to make me cry out against his mouth. I'm vaguely aware of tears wetting my cheeks, but it doesn't matter because nothing matters right now. Nothing but the pleasure coursing through my body in waves, sending me to new heights even as the last bit of my heart remaining shatters into a million pieces.

And then I start sobbing.

Shane manages to get me off his cock and get our clothing righted even though I'm no help at all. I can't stop crying. I don't even know what I'm crying for. As Shane gathers me back into his lap and holds me tightly, words bubble up. "I feel relief that it's over. At some point, I'll be glad we didn't get married. Why does it hurt so much?"

"Endings always hurt, baby girl. Even when they're necessary." He keeps holding me, comforting me with his strength without demanding anything in return. He's content to simply sit there and let me cry. I wish I could say I stop immediately, but even after four days of crying I have enough tears to drown the ocean.

By the time I cry myself out, his shirt is soaked and I don't have to look in a mirror to know that I'm a blotchy mess and all my makeup is gone or smeared beyond repair. It takes longer than it should to realize we're back in the garage, though he hasn't shut it since the truck is still running. I give a hiccupping little sigh. "Sorry."

"Don't be sorry." He tilts my face up, his grip tightening when I try to turn away. "Don't ever apologize to me for what you're feeling." He wipes away my tears, his touch achingly tender. "Come on. Let's get you inside."

I feel a little ridiculous pulling on my panties again, but one look at Shane's face ensures I'm not arguing about it. The second I take my first step out of the truck, I freeze, all thoughts of Max disappearing like a mirage in the desert. Shane opens the door into the house and looks at me, one of his eyebrows arching. "Problem?"

My face is flaming and I can't tell if it's a blush or the aftermath of my sobbing session. "The plug feels funny."

"Mmm." He crooks a finger at me, his amusement deepening as I wiggle a little with each step. "Looks like it's a good kind of funny."

"I think so?"

"Keep it in." He takes the coat off me in the mud room

and hangs it back in its place. Then Shane surveys me. "If you need time—"

I'm already shaking my head. "I don't want to think. Please." When he still hesitates, I move closer. "This started as revenge, but it's—When I'm with you, I'm not thinking about him."

He studies me. "Eventually you have to deal with what you're feeling."

I know that. I desperately wish I didn't know that. I look up at him. "I will. I promise I will. Just…not this weekend."

For a second, I think he's going to keep arguing. He knows this time with him is just a bandage on a bullet wound, but Shane finally catches my hips and pulls me against him. "I'll give you whatever you need."

"Thank you." I'm not even sure what I'm thanking him for. Space. Orgasms. Being here for me to crash myself upon with the minimum damage. No matter how destructive my original impulse to seduce Shane, I can't deny he's caught me in the middle of a freefall. It's still a freefall, but it feels more guided now. I try for a wobbling smile. "I'm going to wash my face."

"Meet me in the kitchen when you're done." He tugs on the loose fabric of the crop top. "Keep this on."

I don't have the energy to push him. Maybe I will in a little bit, but I'm still reeling from the last hour. Good to bad to ugly, a whirlwind of emotions that have left me spinning with no idea which way is up and which is down.

My face is just as bad as I expect. Blotchy skin. Swollen eyes. Black tear tracks down my cheeks. I carefully remove the makeup and spend a few minutes with a cold washcloth over my face. It won't help all that much, but at this point something is better than nothing. I hardly look like the seductress who started this weekend; more like a scared mess of a woman who doesn't know what Monday will bring.

I debate putting on more makeup, but it won't do much good until my skin calms down, and I don't think Shane is going to let me hide up here for over an hour until that happens. I press my hands to my eyes and take a deep breath. I can do this. He's seen me without makeup more often than he's seen me with a full face of it on. I was hardly worried on long pool days when my hair was stiff with chlorine and my nose was sunburned from taking too long to reapply sunscreen.

I also didn't know what Shane's cock tasted like on those days.

Or have a plug in my ass that he put there.

I take a deep breath, smooth down my skirt, and give my hair a toss. That will have to do.

CHAPTER 10

I find him in the little nook connected to the kitchen, setting up a cribbage board, and stop short in the doorway. "What are you doing?"

"It's been a while since we played." Shane shuffles the cards, bridging them in a really satisfying sound that takes me back. Max never enjoyed this game, but my grandfather had taught me as a kid and Shane knew how to play, so we'd spent quite a few evenings in this exact spot while Max watched movies in the living room.

"Shane..." I don't know why I'm hesitating.

He finally looks at me. "We won't talk about him, but there's plenty of other shit we can talk about." His lips quirk up. "Sit down and play with me, Lily."

It seems simple enough, and I find I *do* want to play.

I sit, and immediately jump at how it makes the plug move. Shane grins at me, wickedly delighted. "Problem?"

"You know damn well it's the plug you put up my ass," I mutter, but I can't help smiling a little too. This is too ridiculous. And it doesn't feel *bad*. Just strange. We cut the deck to see who deals first, and it falls to me. As I shuffle, I watch him. "You know, your cock is significantly larger than this plug. If you try to shove it in my ass, you're going to rip me in half."

Shane arches his brows and takes the seat catty-corner to me just like he always does. "You've been fucking the wrong people, Lily. Everything goes smoother when you slow things down. Including my fucking your ass." He says it like it's a sure thing.

I'm not certain he's wrong.

"Uh huh." I deal the cards and we don't speak for a few moments as we get our hands together. Each round of cribbage is split into two parts, and we fall into the rhythm of it as if it hasn't been three months since we played last. "I'm sorry I haven't been around much. Things got hard with..." I stop myself in time. I say I don't want to talk about Max, but he just keeps coming up, making a liar out of me.

Shane lays down his hand and counts out his points, and waits for me to do the same. It's only after I've moved my peg that he says, "How's work going?"

I flash him a grateful smile. "Really, really good. The permanent position at Midway High School has been so great. I feel like I get a lot of support from the principal and the district, and the kids are just... the best. They've been the highlight of the school year."

He shuffles and deals the cards out for the second hand. "They aren't giving you shit?"

"They're high schoolers." I laugh a little. "Of course they give me shit. I'm young and I'm new, and even if I wasn't, it's natural for them to want to test boundaries."

This time, I get more points in the first round, *and* the second round. Shane pushes the cards to me so I can shuffle. "If you were my high school teacher, I wouldn't have been able to focus on shit."

"If I was your high school teacher..." I pretend to think.

"Pretty sure corporeal punishment was allowed back then. I would have smacked the shit out of your hands with a ruler."

Shane glares at me, but he's blatantly fighting not to smile. "I'm forty-seven, Lily. Hardly Grandfather Time."

"I know." A laugh escapes. A real one, loud and freeing. "I promise I know." By the time I deal out the third hand, I'm mostly in control of myself. "And your work? Have you wrapped up that big project?" They'd been working on a new shopping mall in the area, a huge deal for Shane's company to be in charge of.

"Yeah, we got it done right before the holidays."

We chat like that, back and forth as we move through the cribbage board. It's easy. So incredibly easy. I'm a little ashamed at how much relief it gives me to be able to talk freely without twenty layers of hidden meanings the way my conversations with Max had become in the last few months. Neither of us saying what we really meant—unless we were fighting and spitting venom at each other.

"Lily."

I give myself a shake and look at him. "Sorry, I was thinking dark thoughts."

Shane motions to the board. "You just won, baby girl."

I look at my hand on the table and then look at the board. "Oh wow, I guess I did." I don't sound particularly excited, even to my own ears. Damn it, I'm ruining this distraction he created for me. "Sorry, Shane, I—"

"How many times do you think we've played this game? Sitting at this table in these specific spots?"

I blink. "What? I don't know. At least a hundred." Most nights we played more than one, kept going until Max got bored enough to start bitching it was time to leave. A dark part of me wonders if he was texting other women while I was blissfully playing cards with his father.

"Mmhmm." Shane sits back in his chair and looks at me.

"And you've worn that tease of an outfit through at least a few of those times."

I glance down at my clothes. "It's meant as a makeshift swimsuit cover-up."

"Is it?" He moves, fast as a snake, and grabs the bottom of my chair, dragging it to the corner of the table, until my knees bump into his legs under the table and our chairs almost touch. He casually shifts to flip up my skirt, displaying my white panties. "Doesn't look like you're wearing a swimsuit right now."

My skin heats and I nibble my bottom lip. "That's because I'm not."

"Spread your legs."

I force myself to hesitate even though I want to do exactly as he commands. "Shane," I murmur. "We shouldn't."

He looks over my shoulder in the direction of the living room, understanding flashing across his handsome features. "I just want to look, Lily."

I move haltingly, bracing my hands on the chair behind me and slowly spreading my thighs. It takes a little maneuvering to get around the table leg, which means I won't be able to slam them shut. Knowing that makes this hotter. "Like this?"

"Yeah, baby girl, just like that." He exhales slowly as if the sight affects him even now, when he's had me in so many different ways. Almost like this is the first time we've crossed the line. He reaches down and ghosts his hand over my panties. Not *quite* touching, but I swear I can feel the heat of his palm through the lace.

I'm shaking from the need to move, shaking from desire. "You said you were just going to look."

"That's all I'm doing." His gaze meets mine as he draws one knuckle down the center of my panties. "Oops."

"*Shane.*" But I don't try to stop him as he rubs my pussy

through my panties. Just that slow drag of his knuckle over my slit and up to my clit and then back down again. "This isn't what I agreed to."

"Do you want me to stop?"

I make myself look over my shoulder at the doorway into the living room. It doesn't matter that it's empty, that neither of us have said *his* name. We both know what game we're playing. "No," I whisper. "Don't stop." I lick my lips. "It's not like you're really touching me, right? It's just through my panties."

His gaze flares hotter. "That's right, Lily." He roughly palms my pussy, pressing his fingers to my ass where the plug is and making me jump. "I'm not really touching you at all." He pulses his hand, and I have to fight back a moan. "In fact..." Shane reaches up and idly knocks the deck of cards onto the floor at my feet. "Well, fuck. Better pick these up."

I watch with wide eyes as he goes to his knees. He has to push my chair back to make room, and then he's between my thighs, his big hands urging my legs wider. Shane holds my gaze as he presses an open-mouth kiss to my panties. I bite my lip hard to keep a moan inside. "Shane, you promised."

"I'm not touching you." He kisses me again, his tongue tracing my pussy through the lace. "I'm just picking up the damn cards."

I slump back in the chair as he works me with his mouth. We're both so quiet, as if there really is someone else in the house, as if we're half a second from being caught. My panties are soaked, both from my need and from Shane's mouth. "Someone will see."

"Shh." He drags the flat of his tongue over my clit.

"*Shane.*"

"Do you want me to stop?" The arrogant look in his eyes says he knows damn well that I'm half a second from digging my fingers into his hair and riding his face to orgasm.

"No. But… I thought you wanted to look." I can't quite catch my breath. "Don't you want to see what you do to me?"

"Show me." He moved back a few inches, barely enough space for me to get my hand between us.

"Promise you'll only look."

He gives me a long look. "I promise."

Neither of us believe him. I reach down and hook my panties with my finger, towing to them to the side. We both exhale at the sight of my pussy. I'm so wet, I can see it in the fading light of the day. Shane blows out a long breath directly over my clit and this time I can't stop a little moan from slipping free.

"Show me," he growls. "Let me see every bit of that pretty pussy."

I use my free hand to part my pussy, putting myself on full vulgar display for him. "Do you like what you see?"

"Let me have a taste, Lily." He drifts a little closer. "Just a little taste. No one has to know."

"Yes." The word is barely more than a soft exhale, but he hears it all the same. I hold myself open as Shane leans in and drags his tongue over me. "Oh my god." He does it again, and again and then he holds my gaze as he thrusts his tongue into me. "Shane." I'm gasping. "That feels so good."

He rests his forehead on my lower stomach, breathing hard. "Keep saying my name like that, Lily, and I might forget myself and fuck you right here."

Playing with fire. That's all I'm doing with this man. Playing with fucking fire. "Shane," I whisper.

CHAPTER 11

*H*e surges to his feet, catching me around the waist and lifting me onto the table. His dark gaze dares me to protest as he unbuttons the front of his jeans and draws his cock out. "Hold your panties to the side again."

I scramble to obey and shoot a look at the window. We haven't turned on the lights and the setting sun probably has created a mirror of the windows, but that doesn't change the fact that we are in clear view of anyone who's feeling nosy enough to look. "Someone might see."

"What are they going to see?" He drags his cock over me. The broad head of him breaches my entrance. "It hardly counts."

I'm breathing so hard, my breasts are shaking with every exhale. "That's not how it works." I watch him slide another inch into me.

"You sure about that?" He grips my thighs and lifts, pressing them back toward my chest as he sinks deeper. "You're still wearing your panties like a good girl, aren't you?"

If anything, still wearing my panties makes me feel even

sluttier. I try to look innocent and pout a little. "Are you sure? This doesn't feel like I'm being good."

"It doesn't feel good?" He shifts one hand to brush my clit with his thumb. "How about now?"

I squirm. "Wait."

"Wait for what?" He circles my clit again, but doesn't sink the rest of the way into me. "Use your words, Lily."

"I want to be good." I lick my lips. "But I really, really want to be bad, too." When he still doesn't move, I keep talking. "Fuck me on this table, Shane. Please." I glance at the door to the living room. "Just be quiet."

"I'm not the one who's going to have to be quiet." He presses me flat on the table and covers my mouth with a big hand. The pressure against my lips makes me moan as much as him forcing his cock the rest of the way into me. He felt impossibly big in the truck with the addition of the plug, but somehow it's even more intense in this position. "You can tell yourself that you don't want this, that it doesn't count, but we both know the truth." He leans down and his lips brush my ear. "You've been looking for an excuse to climb on my cock since the day we met."

I make a sound that might be protest, but it doesn't matter because he's fucking me in long strokes. He barely pauses to guide my hands to my thighs, forcing me to hold them wide and even closer to my chest. I try to keep the waves of pleasure at bay. I really do. I pull his palm off my mouth enough to say, "Hurry. We have to be quick." Then I go back to holding myself open for him.

Shane clamps his hand around my jaw and his expression goes hard. "You've been denying me this pussy, Lily, but it's mine now. I'll fuck you as fast or slow as I want. Do you hear me?"

"Yes," I whisper.

"You clamp around my cock every time I remind your

71

pussy who it belongs to." He keeps thrusting, keeps imprinting the feel of him into my very soul. "You like it when I get possessive."

I want to deny it. This feels like a different kind of dangerous. But I can't deny the truth. "I like feeling owned by you."

Shane's expression changes, something flickering in those dark eyes that I can't put a name to. "I should finish inside you, should send you back to him all filled up with my come."

"Do it," I challenge.

"No." He pulls out of me and hits his knees in front of the table. He wraps his fist around the crotch of my panties and drags them down my legs. "I'm keeping these."

"Wait—"

"No shields, Lily." He looks up at me. "You might be a little slut for wanting my mouth on you, but you're *my* good girl. And my good girl asks for what she wants."

Pleasure thrills through me. "Make me come, Daddy."

He doesn't immediately close the distance between us. "You're going to orgasm all over my face, and then I'm going to fuck that pretty mouth until you swallow me down."

It's not quite a question, but I'm already nodding. "Yes. Please, yes. That's what I want."

And then his mouth is on me again. I don't think I'll ever get enough of how much Shane loves eating my pussy. He fucking *savors* it, like I'm a fine wine and he's determined to pick up all the notes like I'm his favorite treat. For once, he's not teasing me. He's going after me like my pleasure is his to command, like my next orgasm is the only thing he wants. I come so hard I lose my balance and smack back onto the table. He lifts his head in surprise, but I dig my fingers into his hair and tow him back down. "Just a little more. Please, Daddy."

Shane chuckles against my heated flesh. "Greedy girl."

"Yes."

Even though it wasn't what he promised, he works me up again, slower this time, until I'm quivering and whimpering, and begging him to finish me off. Shane pushes a single finger into me and strokes my G-spot. "I'm going to fuck your ass tonight, Lily."

I'm so out of my mind, my earlier apprehension feels like a thousand miles away. "Do it. I don't care. Do it now. Just let me come."

He sucks hard on my clit and then he gives me what I need, my orgasm so intense I forget to breathe for several long moments, only managing a harsh inhale at last moment. "Holy shit."

Shane pulls me up and gathers me to him, holding me close as I ease back into my body. "Holy shit," I repeat. "Do you think you can die from sex being too good? Because I think I might be dying."

His rough laugh makes me shiver. Shane shifts back enough to gently clasp my chin and lift my face to his. He kisses me, the barest brushing of his mouth to mine. "You say that now, but in about thirty seconds, you'll be begging for more."

"I don't know." I cling to him, his steadiness soothing something inside me. "It's never been like this before. It's never even been close."

He releases my chin and tucks my head in against his shoulder. "It's never been like this for me, either."

Alarms try to blare through my head, a warning that we're both in deep and sinking fast, but I can't make myself care. Maybe we were always in too deep and this weekend is only showcasing exactly how fucked we are. "Shane…"

This time he doesn't interrupt me, doesn't distract me. He just waits. If I was stronger, I'd tell him about the complicated feelings in my chest, the ones that signal that this is anything but a simple revenge fuck. I'm not strong though. I'm a coward.

I nudge him back a step and slide down to my knees in front of him. Something akin to disappointment flickers over his face before he runs his fingers through my hair and shifts it to wrap around his left fist. He wraps his other hand around his cock and taps it to my bottom lip. "Open."

This isn't like in the truck earlier. He let me suck his dick then. Now he's fully intending on fucking my mouth.

"One day, I want to see your lips painted a pretty pink and wrapped around my cock." He thrusts slowly, letting me adjust as much as I'm able to. "This, though? This is fucking perfection, baby girl." He hesitates. "It gets to be too much, you slap my thigh. Do you understand?"

He allows me to withdraw enough to answer. "Yes, Daddy." I should leave it at that, but I can't. "It won't be too much."

His dark laugh is the only warning I get before he starts moving again. Where before, he was easing me in, because he's so damn careful with me, now he's using me to get himself off. Using my mouth.

He's too big, too long, just too fucking much. He's barely halfway in when he's triggering my gag reflex. "Use your hand, Lily." He barely slows down to allow me to obey, gagging me just the tiniest bit with every stroke, his expression downright ferocious as if daring me to protest. I fist my hand around his cock.

I almost panic. I can't breathe with him filling me, can't control anything, can't stop him from going too far...

And just like that, a switch flips in my brain and I stop fighting him. I relax entirely into what he's doing, letting him in deeper, letting him control everything. It allows him another precious inch or two, but he looks like I just gave him a priceless gift. "That's right, baby girl. Trust me. Take me deep."

I move my fist as a counterpoint to the way he fucks my mouth, driven on by his low curses and moans. He looks *pained* as he stares down at me. "Jesus Christ, Lily. Sweet fuck, suck me harder. I'm close."

I obey. I'm helpless to do anything but exactly what he wants me to. When he comes, I swallow him down, sucking his cock even as his grip loosens and it's more like he's hanging on for support than trying to hold me in place. He finally drags me off his cock with a curse and watches me with an almost strained expression as I lick my lips.

"You might not be the only one who dies from fucking." Shane pulls me to my feet and kisses me hard. We taste like each other, like the dirtiest kind of fucking, like the promise of more. He finally releases me and tucks his cock back in his pants, but the way his gaze skates over me says he's considering another plan of attack. "Seeing you in that tiny skirt and knowing I can slip my hand under it whenever I want is addicting, Lily." He does exactly as he says, palming me under my skirt. "I can't get enough," he murmurs, almost as if he's talking to himself. He wedges two fingers into me and then goes still as if savoring the way I feel. "You make me feel like I'm eighteen and just want to fuck and fuck and fuck."

I release a shuddering breath. "I feel like that with you, too."

"You need to eat something."

"I'm really not hungry."

For some reason, that makes him shake his head. He withdraws his fingers slowly, reluctantly, and then smooths down my skirt as if making sure everything is in its place. Then he holds my gaze as he sucks his fingers into his mouth and cleans me off him.

"Fuck," I breathe. "Why is that so hot?"

"Because it's us." He walks to the sink to wash his hands and then moves to the fridge. "Why don't you go watch some TV? This will be a little bit."

It's not exactly a command, but it sounds firmer than a suggestion. "Yes, Daddy," I say primly and then walk out while he's still cursing.

CHAPTER 12

J don't mean to fall asleep on the couch. One second I'm watching my favorite slasher film on demand, and the next I'm vaguely aware of Shane picking me up and carrying me upstairs. I barely manage to open my eyes as he pulls my clothes off, and guides me onto my stomach to ease the plug out. "Sorry," I manage.

"You need the rest." He disappears for a few moments, and then returns to tuck us into his bed.

I'm barely awake enough to register disappointment that apparently we're just sleeping now, him wrapping his big body around me, before darkness sucks me under once more. I don't dream, which is a relief in and of itself.

I open my eyes to the morning light streaming through the windows and Shane's comforting weight next to me. It takes several long moments for the sounds I'm hearing to penetrate, and another few before my mind is functioning well enough to focus on him sitting against the headboard. On how he has my phone in his hand. On the way his other hand is beneath the sheets bunched at his waist, moving rhythmically.

"Shane."

"Mmm." He looks at me, but doesn't make a move to stop what he's doing.

I sit up. "Are you jacking off right next to me? With *my* phone?"

"Come here." He stops stroking himself and pulls me to sit on his lap, my back to his chest. "We didn't get around to watching this yesterday."

I don't ask how he has the code to my phone. I've never been particularly stealthy when unlocking it, and this man misses nothing. Instead, I settle back against him as he presses play again and I'm confronted with the video of his fingers in my pussy. I've seen it a number of times at this point in real life, but somehow in the video it looks even filthier. His fingers are *soaked*, my wetness coating them. Then the angle changes and he's shoving those same fingers into my mouth.

I barely recognize myself.

This video version of me taking his fingers as he grips my chin looks like... I shift in his lap. "I really do look like a dirty little slut."

"It gets better," he growls against my neck.

The phone moves. This is where I went to get condoms, and I watch as Shane sets it on the couch and adjusts the angle before taking his seat. "How many times have you watched this while you waited for me to wake up?" I whisper.

"A few." His hand skates over my hip and down to cup my pussy. "Sore?"

"Yes." I spread my legs a bit more. "But I don't care. I'll take anything you give me today." Because it's the last day. The last night. Tomorrow this ends, and I'm desperately afraid it's already too late for me. It's going to hurt to walk away and never seen Shane again, but what am I supposed to do? Max and I need a clean break. If I keep fucking Shane, eventually I'll see Max again and that's…

In the phone, I come back into the frame and there's some shuffling as he rolls the condom on. As dirty as it felt to be riding his cock that first time, it looks even dirtier. Even in the freaking phone camera, I can see how big he is, how wet it gets me as I ride him. I watch his cock disappear into my pussy, watch my body roll sensuously as I ride him. "I look really hot."

Shane chuckles and presses a finger into my pussy. I *am* sore, but I'm too turned on to care. He pumps slowly. "You like watching yourself."

"I like watching us." I try to hold still, try to focus on the video and not on lifting my hips to meet his hand. "I wasn't sure when you said you wanted to record it, but this? This is sexy as hell."

The recording of us switches positions and I meet my own gaze in the phone. I look completely unrepentant, so out of my mind that I don't give a damn that I'm completely on display—that I'm actually *into* being on display. "I like watching you fuck me."

"Mmm." He just keeps up those slow strokes, as if he can do this all day.

We watch in silence for the rest of the video, and then I swipe to the next one. I squirm on his finger at the sight of him spreading my pussy and his tongue flicking over my clit, but it's the way he watches me in the video that really does a number on me. The man looks at me like I'm his. Not just in sexy playacting. Actually his. As if he's wanted this for so long, he can't fucking believe he's gotten it, and he's not going to let it go without a fight.

That was only the *first night*.

I swipe again and there's the picture of him with that

79

exact expression in his eyes, with his mouth all over my pussy. "This one's my favorite."

"Mine, too."

Pleasure builds in slow waves. I lean my head back against his shoulder. "Do you want me to send them to you?"

"Not yet."

I twist a little to look at him. "What do you mean not yet?"

"Not yet," he repeats. Shane sets me on the bed and then moves down to settle between my thighs. "It occurs to me that I promised to wake you up with my mouth, and I've failed on that count twice now."

I take a slow breath and release the tiny flicker of frustration at him dodging my question. This is what I'm here for, after all. Orgasms. Fucking. Not to pepper him with questions that have nothing to do with either. Except... It was his idea to film us. Why doesn't he want a copy of the videos?

Shane's mouth scatters my thoughts like bowling pins. Once again, he's treating this like the main event, like he could lick and kiss and tongue-fuck me all day and be completely satisfied with only that. I whimper and dig my fingers into his hair. "I love the way you eat my pussy. It's like you never want to stop."

"I can't get enough of you, baby girl," he murmurs against me. "Your taste is like a fucking drug. I *don't* ever want to stop." He circles my clit with the tip of his tongue, making me moan. "And when you sound like that? I could draw those sounds from you all fucking day."

And then there's no more air for talking. I expect him to tease me like he has before, to push me to the edge and then back off again and again. This morning is different. Shane's going after my pussy like my orgasms are a secondary benefit. Like this is all for him and if I come, I come, because he's not going to stop.

By my second orgasm, I'm panting. I try to shove his face away, but he just shifts a little to the side, leaving my over-sensitized clit alone and sucking and licking my pussy lips. "Oh my god, *Shane*. You're going to kill me. I can't—"

"You can take more," he growls. He bands an arm over my hips, pinning me in place as he winds me up again. "You're going to take as much as I decide to give you."

I barely register when my grip on his hair goes from trying to get him off me to trying to get him closer. Time has no meaning right now. I lift my hips, but he holds me down, only making it hotter. "Shane, please."

He ignores me, intent on tracing every inch of me with his tongue as if trying to memorize me. I shiver and shake and then I'm coming again, my heels digging into the mattress and a shriek escaping my lips. "Oh, *fuck*."

Still, he doesn't stop.

"Shane…" I whimper. I can't think, can't fucking focus. "Please Daddy." I'm almost sobbing. "Just a little break."

"You need this cock, baby girl?"

I don't know if I can take that any more than I can take his mouth his mouth right now, but I'm already nodding. "Yes. Please, yes."

He crawls up my body and guides his cock into me. Shane gathers me to him and fucks me slowly. The man holds me like he cares about me. I was wrong. This doesn't feel like fucking. This slow slide of his cock, his face buried in my neck, his hands holding me so damn close… It feels like a whole lot more than sex.

I love it.

I soak it up like the best kind of alcohol, not caring that it will hurt in the end. I want it now. I want *him*. "Kiss me," I gasp.

He lifts his head and takes my mouth. This, too, feels like we're communicating on a level beyond words. Like he's telling me something and I'm answering and neither of us can pretend otherwise. I'm lost in a sea of pleasure, clinging to him as each stroke pushes us farther and farther toward something we can't take back, my stupid broken heart in my throat. It's a good thing his tongue steals my words before I can give them voice, because unforgivable sentences spill together inside my head.

Keep me.

Please keep me.

I think I might love you.

They wash away as I come, further disperse as he follows me over the edge. We lay there for a long time, the sweat cooling on our bodies, our breathing slow easing back to normal, and still he doesn't move. I stroke my hands down his back and whimper when he thrusts into me a little. "Oh god, that feels good and also not good and you're going to make me come again."

Shane, the bastard, does it again. "I can't get enough of you, Lily." He's said it before, but it feels different now. Like a promise instead of another flavor of dirty talk. He thrusts a third time. It doesn't matter that he's only half hard in me. It's like my body is already poised after so much pleasure, like it's unable to stop.

I writhe under him, nearly mindless. "Why can't I stop?" I whine. "It's too much."

"I know." He kisses me as he thrusts. Drinking me down even as we grind together, mindless and frenzied.

I grab his ass and pull him tighter against me, lifting my hips to work myself on him. "Yes. Right there. I'm so close."

"Use me, baby girl. Get yourself off. Once more and you can rest."

Pleasure short-circuits what's left of my brain. Words pour out and this time his mouth isn't there to catch them. "I hate you. Oh god, I love you. I don't fucking know, just..." I cry out as I orgasm. I might actually black out. It sure as hell seems like it because one second I'm writhing on his cock and the next he's on his back and I'm sprawled across his chest, his arms clasping me to him. I think I might be crying again. I don't know if it's tears or sweat, but I'm wrung out. Gloriously empty.

Shane kisses the top of my head and yanks the covers back over us. If I had a bone left in my body, I might tense as I wait for him to say something. But he doesn't. He just idly strokes my back as I recover. The silence isn't exactly uncomfortable, but I can't get my words out of my head.

I hate you. I love you.

Only one of those is true. And it's not the simpler option.

CHAPTER 13

I close my eyes. It might not be possible to die from too many orgasms, but I'm pretty sure it *is* possible to die from humiliation. "Please say something."

"You need to eat."

That surprises me enough that I lift my head to look at him. "What?"

"You passed out before we had dinner last night, and you barely had a snack for lunch. Breakfast this morning is non-negotiable." He studies my face. "You haven't slept much, either, since you found out what he did."

I can feel my face heating with something like guilt. "I think I can be forgiven having a stress response to finding out my fiancé is fucking his secretary." Not just fucking. Dating. I'd almost forgotten. My stomach twists in knots at the reminder. "For me, that means I don't sleep much and sometimes I forget to eat. It'll pass."

Shane doesn't seem the least bit happy with my response. "That's bullshit. You choose not to take care of yourself."

"That's about enough of that." I sit up, but I only make it that far before he's got me pinned to the bed, his big body wedged between my legs. I glare at his throat, refusing to meet his gaze. "I'll eat breakfast, okay? Let me up."

"Lily." He sounds so severe that I shiver. "Look at me."

I don't want to. I want to squeeze my eyes shut and ignore whatever he's about to say. I can't deny him, though. I've lost the ability somewhere along the way in the last two days. Slowly, oh so slowly, I meet his gaze. "Happy?"

"No, I'm not fucking happy. I see what he's done to you and what you're doing to yourself in response. Do you think it's going to hurt him if you hurt yourself?"

I flinch. "That's not what I'm aiming for."

"You sure about that?" His brows draw together. "You know what goes with sleep loss and lack of food? Things get muddled in your head. You think you're going to be the teacher those kids need when you're not taking care of yourself because you're so busy crying over some guy who didn't deserve you."

Oh, bringing my students into this is a low blow. I can't fight that argument, because I know he's right, so I focus on the one thing I *do* have a response to. "Some guy. You sure don't have much nice to say about your own fucking son right now."

"No, I don't." He doesn't flinch, doesn't look away. "You can throw him in my face if you want, but it doesn't change anything."

"I might like you being my Daddy, but I already have a father."

His expression goes positively forbidding. "Your father might not spank you anymore, but I won't hesitate to paddle your ass if I think you need it."

I'm breathing hard, but I can't tell if it's because I'm furious or turned on. "Fuck you, Shane."

"There goes that mouth again." He sits back. I try to push him off, but he's too gloriously strong. He flips me onto my stomach with ease and drags me to the edge of the mattress. Once again, I try to straighten, and just like he did yesterday morning, he pins me down with a hand at the back of my neck.

"Don't you fucking dare!"

His hand comes down hard on my ass. I barely have a chance to process the sting when he hits my other cheek. I shriek in fury. But the pain gets all tangled up in my head and I'm fighting not to grind against the edge of the mattress as he spanks me again. A fourth time, and my breath is sobbing from my throat.

Shane massages my ass, which makes things both better and worse. "Someone has to take care of you, baby girl. You obviously can't be trusted to do it yourself."

I fist the comforter and bite my bottom lip hard. I'll be damned before I beg him to touch me. But I can't help widening my stand the tiniest bit. A silent question.

He gives a dark chuckle. "Look at you. You want my fingers inside you and you can't even bring yourself to ask me. You're doing a hell of a job of proving my point."

"I am *exceedingly* angry with you right now," I grind out.

"I bet." His thumb starts at the small of my back and traces down to where I wore the plug yesterday. He circles me. "You'll wear the plug again today."

"Shane—"

His breath ghosts across my smarting flesh, and then he kisses the lower curve of my ass. "You want to be a good girl, don't you, Lily?"

I want to tell him to fuck off again, but I like what he's doing too much to risk him stopping. And, even more, something in me goes soft as he moves to my other cheek, soothing the still-stinging ass. "Yes, Daddy," I whisper.

He rises without giving me what I want. "Get ready and meet me downstairs."

I straighten awkwardly and stumble into the bathroom without looking at him. I have the most ridiculous urge to cry again, but I can't even begin to say why. I've already come so many times this morning, I don't know if I can take more even if he was willing.

My pussy aches. My ass hurts. My fucking heart is a murky mess.

I take my time getting ready, take even longer in the shower as if I can wash away the very memory of him. It's an impossible task, even if I wanted to purge the memories. He's imprinted on my very skin.

Once I'm dried off, I turn and look at my ass in the mirror. It's bright red and I can already tell there will be bruises. I should be angry about that, but the knowledge that I'll wear his marks even after we're done makes me smile a little. Complicated. This whole thing is so fucking complicated.

In the bedroom, I find a sundress, white with pink flowers. It's short and flirty and Shane didn't bother to add underwear to the list. Probably because the white pair was the only one I left here and he's decided to keep them.

I check myself in the mirror. This is another dress I wore as a swimsuit cover up, the top triangles exposing plenty of the curves of my breasts, the length just shy of indecent. I feel positively sinful knowing I'm naked beneath it.

One more day.

I only have one more day with Shane, and I'm going to make it count.

I head downstairs and find him cooking a full spread. Eggs and bacon and what appear to be homemade hash browns. Despite the fact I would have said I wasn't hungry, my stomach grumbles at the delicious smells.

Like yesterday, he barely glances as me as he pulls a plate out of the oven and sets it on the table. "It's hot."

"Shane…"

"Eat, Lily. Before I lose my patience."

I raise my brows. Someone's still pissed about earlier. Fine. I'm hungry, so I'll eat. Then he can yell at me some more if it will make him feel better. Maybe I'll get on my knees and offer to suck his cock in penance. The thought makes me smile a little as I dig into the food he prepared.

We eat in silence, and then Shane does the dishes. I try to help, but he points at the chair in a silent command to sit. It feels more like a punishment than I expect, because all I'm left to do is sit and watch him. He looks freaking *good*. His jeans are faded from countless washings and hug his ass and thighs in a comfortable sexy sort of way, and his shoulders fill out his equally faded T-shirt. The fabric is so thin, it pulls against the muscles in his back each time he reaches forward to grab another dish.

By the time he's moved on to drying—fucking *hand drying* —I'm clenching my thighs together. When I shift, my ass aches worse, which only makes me hotter. So I keep doing it, shamelessly driving my need higher.

He finishes and turns around, the towel slung over his shoulder. Shane glances at me and shakes his head. "Stand up. Let's get a look at you."

This inspection feels as strange as the one did yesterday. *He* picked out my clothes, but he's acting like it's still up for debate whether he approves of them.

A tempting thought flickers through my head before I can banish it. Of what it would be like if this was *every* morning. If we shared breakfast and then he examined my clothing to see if he approved. Maybe it shouldn't feel so sexy, but it sure as hell does.

Shane circles me, finally coming to stop in front of me. He's frowning, which sends a delicious bolt of lust through me. "Lily, what am I going to do with you?"

I can think of a few things, but I affect an innocent expression. "Is something wrong, Daddy?"

He flicks a finger easily sliding the thin strap of my dress off my shoulder. It drops down my arm and the dress sags on that side, exposing my bare breast. Shane shakes his head. "Little slut." He cups my breast, coasting his thumb back and forth across my nipple. "How many times are you planning on flashing people today?"

"Um." I can't stop watching his hand on my breast, his thumb stroking the hardened peak of my nipple. It feels dirtier because I still have the rest of my dress on, like a secret just between us. "I'm sorry?"

"I might believe you if that sentence didn't have a question mark at the end." He casually pulls my second strap off and my dress falls to my waist. Shane cups my other breast, giving it the same treatment. "You have magnificent breasts, Lily. Has anyone ever told you that?"

I can't quite catch my breath. "I usually get the 'nice tits' comment."

He snorts. "Idiots. You've fucked nothing but idiots." He dips down and presses an open-mouthed kiss to the curve of my right breast before moving to the nipple. "These deserve to be worshiped just like the rest of you." I start to lift my hands and he stops, giving me a severe look. "Hold still until I'm finished examining you."

I drop my hands, my face flaming. He moves to my other breast and gives it the same slow, thorough treatment. Shane lifts his head and exhales across my wet skin, raising goosebumps. "Lift your dress, Lily. Show me if you decided to be a good girl or a little slut today."

I comply with shaking hands. Shane goes to his knees, his brows drawn together. "Lily." The warning in his voice makes me shiver. "We talked about this."

"Sorry, Daddy." I widen my stance, just a little. "I thought you might want dessert."

He barks out a laugh and grins at me, the sheer force of his amusement nearly bowling me over. Just like that, Shane locks it down, but mirth still dances in his dark eyes. "Positively shameless."

"Guilty." I glance out the kitchen window. "Oh look, your neighbors are outside again." I smirk down at him. "Better get off your knees before they think you have your mouth all over my pussy in here."

"Turn around and put your hands on the counter." His command slaps me and I obey before I can stop and think of a reason not to. Shane's big hands grip my thighs, pushing them wide as he flips up my dress to bunch around my hips. I might as well be naked for all that it covers me. "I had you like this yesterday, and I didn't let you come."

"I remember," I whisper.

His hands coast up until his thumbs brush my pussy. "Just this morning you begged me to stop eating you out."

"I remember that, too." I arch my back, offering myself to him. "I won't beg again."

"Oh, baby girl." His breath ghosts over my pussy. "Yes, you will."

CHAPTER 14

Shane starts slow. Like he's doing this for the first time. Like he wants to memorize me. He parts my pussy with his thumbs, ensuring he doesn't miss a bit of me. It's not designed to make me come, just to tease me, to put a delicious melting feeling in my body.

I lay my cheek on the counter and give myself over to him completely. I feel like a temptress, like I've brought this powerful man to his knees. "I'm a terrible person, Daddy."

His finger replaces his mouth, pushes into me agonizingly slowly. "That so?"

"Yes." I spread my legs wider and shift back to take his finger deeper. "I get off on thinking about the look on his face if he came into the kitchen right now and saw us."

Shane's silent for several long moments, his finger moving in me. "Would you like that, Lily? Would it make you feel good?"

I stare out the window at his normal neighbors going about their normal lives. "I don't know. It feels good to be bad with you. I don't know where my lines are any more."

"Don't move." Shane's finger disappears and it's everything I can do not to sob out a protest. I can hear him moving behind me, but I'm content to wait for what comes next, to let him have full control. Even so, I jump when something cool and wet spreads down my crack. A second later, he spreads my cheeks and the metal plug presses against me. "Relax, Lily." As I obey, he eases it into me. "How does that feel?"

"Better than I thought it would." Despite his giant fucking cock, I'm actually looking forward to him taking my ass tonight. If I trust any man to ensure I have a good time doing anal, it's Shane. The thought makes me laugh a little.

"Something funny?"

"Even when I was fantasizing about you, I never went that far. I never thought about you in my ass."

"Mmm." His finger traces the plug. "I've thought about it. I've thought about fucking every part of you, Lily. In a thousand different ways. You're like a sickness in my blood."

"Gee, thanks."

He gives my ass a light slap and I jump. Then I moan when the sharp move and tiny flicker of pain make the plug feel hotter. Shane goes back to massaging my ass cheeks like he can't get enough of the way I fill his hands. "You make me want to do depraved things to your tight little body."

"Do them," I moan.

But he just keeps touching me, his rough hands making my smarting cheeks feel agonizingly sensitized. "I have a suggestion. Don't say yes if you don't want to."

I try to focus on his words and not on his touch. "I'm listening."

"We make another video. For him."

My eyes go wide. "Shane," I say slowly. "You want to make a revenge sex tape to send to your son?"

"You decide if it ever gets sent." He eases my dress back

down. "Could be that having the video will satisfy your need to get caught, to hurt him."

Honestly, it's not a half bad idea. I don't know if I really *want* Max to catch us, but the dangerous impulse is there all the same. Maybe if we play it out, it will diffuse.

I slowly stand and turn. Shane's gaze goes to my breasts, but he just tucks my dress back up on my shoulders, covering me. I swallow hard. "If we do it, we pretend it's the first time."

"Lily, you're wearing my plug in your ass right now."

I shiver. "So?

He shakes his head. "Yeah, okay. We play this however you need."

I look around. I'm not sure the best way to go about it. The possibilities make me nearly giddy. We could fuck anywhere in the house, could play out this little revenge fantasy however we want. "Um, where?"

"Go get your phone."

I hurry upstairs and grab my phone. For the first time, it strikes me that I don't have a single message or call from Max. We're done and he doesn't even care about trying to talk about it. I don't know what there is to say, but it feels so shitty to know that he's with *her* and if I hadn't thrown caution to the wind and come to Shane, I'd be huddled up in my apartment, sobbing myself sick over him.

I find Shane in the living room. The morning sunlight streams in from the back windows, the snow on the ground amplifying the brightness. He stands at the entertainment center and motions me over when I walk into the room. I hand over my phone and watch as he sets it up at the base of the television. "Go sit on the couch," he says.

I do, watching as he makes some adjustments. Shane glances at me. "Talk for a second. Let's see how the sound is."

I raise my brows. "I am really, really looking forward to riding your cock, Daddy."

He gives me a long look. "Maybe I'll just bend you over the arm of the couch and fuck you like the dirty girl you are."

I clench my thighs together. "Maybe I'll like it."

"You will." He says it like there was never any other outcome. "You love everything I do to you."

There's no use arguing that. I wait while he plays back the short video and nods. "This will do. Go to the front door."

I push to my feet and obey, making a quick detour to the mud room to grab my heels. I wait in the entranceway, my heart in my throat, as he walks to me with heavy steps. Confusion pulls his brows together. "Lily, what are you doing here?"

Show time. "I didn't know where else to go."

He hesitates, and it *feels* real. Like he knows I shouldn't be here, but he doesn't want me to leave. "Come in." Shane leads me into the living room and guides me to sit on the same cushion I'd just occupied. Even though I know the name of this game, I still shift a little nervously as he takes the spot right next to me, his knees bumping into mine. He gives me a concerned look. "Tell me what's going on."

"Max and I are done." My breath catches in my throat, but I push on. "I, uh, I found him with his secretary. It's over. The wedding is off. The whole nine yards."

"Fuck, I'm sorry." He truly looks like he means it.

"I just…" To my horror, my bottom lip quivers. I press my hand to my mouth. "I'm sorry. I shouldn't have come. I know he's your son and—"

Shane pulls me into his arms. The hug is a little awkward, made more awkward when he shifts back a little and my legs get tangled with his. The plug in my ass gives lie to the newness of this, but it still *feels* forbidden. Like he's offering me comfort and didn't mean to put us in a position where my dress is riding up to indecent heights.

His hand drops to my thigh and he flinches. "Jesus, I'm sorry." But he doesn't quite take his touch away, his fingers lingering on my skin.

"It's okay." I lean back a little, but not enough for it to be a real retreat. "I…" I don't want to share the same story from before, where he watched me masturbate in the back yard. That moment feels like it was just for us, and I don't want to mar it.

Instead, I shift against him, sliding my leg higher up between his. It almost looks like I'm trying to get my balance to move away, but his hand catches me high on my thigh, his big fingers curving around beneath. It's not *quite* indecent, but he's in a position to guess I might not be wearing anything underneath this dress.

I look up at him with wide eyes. "Shane?"

He holds my gaze as he slides his hand higher, under my dress, up over my hip, my ass. "Lily, why did you come to my house without panties on?"

"Um." I'm fisting his T-shirt and I can't seem to stop shaking. "I don't know."

"You don't know?" His tone is faintly mocking. He smooths his hand over my ass and down the back of my thigh, hooking me behind my knee and pulling my leg higher up around his waist. Cool air touches my pussy and I have to fight back a moan.

I don't mean to kiss him. I don't think? But I tilt my face up and then his mouth is on mine. Plundering me, forcing my lips wide and slipping his tongue into my mouth, kissing me until I'm writhing against him. Shane barely touches me, one hand on my knee, holding me in place, the other at the small of my back, but it doesn't matter. I rub against him and my dress slides off my shoulders, shifts up higher on my hips.

I lean back and his gaze snags on my mostly bared breasts. "Lily." God, I love it when he talks to me like that. Like I'm being bad and he's not amused.

"I'm sorry." I shift back a little and try to fix my dress with fumbling hands. "Sorry I kissed you. That was inappropriate." I go still and then shake my head. "You know what? I'm not sorry. You're sexy as hell, Shane, and I'd be lying if I said I don't want you."

His brows rise. "You were engaged to my son a few short days ago."

"Yes, I was." I move to straddle his lap, and he lets me. I lean down and brush my lips to his ear. The rest of what we're doing is for the camera. These words are just for us. "Wouldn't a good daughter-in-law want to make her Daddy feel good?" I shift against his chest, letting my dress drop again. "Wouldn't a caring father-in-law want to kiss his baby girl and make it better?"

"You and that dirty fucking mouth," he murmurs. His hands land on my hips, urging me back, but it's like his senses get crisscrossed when he sees my breasts. He freezes and it's like we're both holding our breath as he leans in and rubs his face against my sensitive skin, taking first one nipple and then the other into his mouth.

"Oh god, that feels good." I dig my fingers into his hair and arch my back. He slides his hands up the back of my thighs to my ass, massaging there beneath my dress. Again, the plug heightens the sensation, until I'm fighting not to writhe in his lap. I tug his hair. "We should stop. This isn't why I came here. This is wrong."

"I know." He lifts me and turns us around, sitting me on the couch and going to his knees on the floor. "We'll stop in a minute. Just... Just a minute." He shoves up my dress and then his mouth is on me.

I moan. "Shane." I'm lifting my hips to meet his tongue,

shamelessly holding my legs wide open as he licks me. "Shane, you're my father-in-law. You shouldn't be... We shouldn't be..." I shudder as he sticks his tongue deep inside me. "It feels so dirty to have your mouth all over me."

He sucks lightly on my clit. "I'll stop in a minute. Just a little longer."

I'm already nodding. "Just a little longer. We can stop in a minute."

He goes back to eating my pussy in slow, thorough kisses. Need quivers up my legs, made more intense by the picture I know we paint. Him fully clothed and on his knees. Me with my dress bunched around my waist, somehow more naked than if I had nothing else on. "What if he sees?"

He barely lifts his head. "You mean what if Max walked in on us with my mouth all over your pussy?"

"Yes," I moan.

He pushes two fingers into me. "Then my asshole son would finally see what you look like when you come."

My jaw drops, but he doesn't give me a chance to answer. Shane already knows my body, knows the quickest way to wind me up and get me off. He strokes those two wide fingers against my G-spot as he works my clit with this lips and tongue. I let my head fall back against the couch. "Oh *fuck*. Don't stop. That feels so fucking good, Shane. You're going to make me come if you don't stop."

He doesn't stop. He just drives me slowly, inexorably over the edge, until I'm shaking and sobbing out each exhale and coming all over his face. He gives me one last long lick and finally lifts his head. I grab his face and tow him up to me, moaning at the taste of myself on his lips. "Get your cock out. Get it out right now."

"No."

He takes advantage of my surprise and hauls me forward over his shoulder. "If I'm going to fuck that pretty pussy of yours, Lily. I'm damn well going to do it right." My world goes upside down as he stands and walks down the hall and up to his bedroom. He drops me on the bed. "Get on your hands and knees. Spread your thighs and show me how wet I just made that pussy."

I scramble to obey. Playacting was hot, but this is *us*. I hold myself up with one hand and slip the other between my thighs to spread my pussy. Shane's rough curse makes me grin. Didn't expect *that*, did he?

"No matter how many times you come, it's still not enough, is it? Your pussy is greedy for more." I can hear him rustling behind me as he strips. "Finger yourself. Show me how wet you are."

"Yes, Daddy." I slip my middle finger into myself. It feels a thousand times better knowing he's watching. "I'm so wet."

"I can see that." But his footsteps move away. I almost turn to look, but he returns a few moments later and the mattress gives as he climbs onto the bed. He knocks my hand away and then his cock is there, pushing into me. "I'm going to fuck your virgin ass, Lily. Are you ready for that?"

I don't know if I'm ready, but I nod against the mattress. "Yes, Daddy."

CHAPTER 15

*S*hane keeps thrusting as if he's got nowhere better to be than balls deep inside me. "I like watching my cock disappear into your pussy while that plug teases about how full your ass is. It feels good to be full, doesn't it, baby girl?"

"Yes," I moan.

His voice is pure sin. "Almost like being fucked by two cocks." He spreads my cheeks and then he's shifting the plug, easing it in and out of me. "But you don't get two cocks, my little slut. You get mine, and it will be enough because I'm your fucking Daddy."

I'm writhing on his cock with nowhere to go. "Please fuck my ass. Please."

And then the plug is gone and he's easing out of me. He presses something to my hand and I blink at the wand vibrator. "Use this when I tell you." He urges my hips up. "Relax."

"You relax when you're about to have a giant cock in your ass," I mutter.

He gives my ass a light slap and then he's spreading lube all over me. I instinctively tense as the feeling of the broad head of his cock. Shane smooths one hand over my hip and up my back. "Relax, baby girl. Trust me."

I try to obey. I expect pain as the head of his cock eases past my entrance, and it *does* burn a bit, but it's nowhere near the level I thought it would be. I shift a little and Shane's hand tightens on my hip. "Easy."

"More," I demand.

He eases in a bit more and gives a slow, short thrust. "We good?"

I didn't expect to like this. I really didn't. I should know better by now. It's completely different than when he's in my pussy, but it feels weirdly good. "More," I say again.

"Use the vibrator."

It takes me a second to get it on and then I position the broad head of it against my clit. "Oh fuck."

"Mmm." He has both hands on my ass now, holding me open as he slowly penetrates me. "We're almost there, baby girl. You feel so fucking good."

"You do, too." I have to fight not to writhe. "I'm going to come with your cock in my ass like a little slut, aren't I?"

Shane's hips meet my ass and he exhales slowly. "Yes. That's exactly what you're going to do." He bears me down to the mattress, his big body covering mine. He kisses the back of my neck, my shoulder, my spine. "You are so fucking perfect, Lily. I said you were a gift, but that doesn't begin to cover it." He starts to fuck my ass. It's nowhere near as rough as he's been literally every time we've had sex, but it feels like I'm being invaded over and over again. I flick the vibrator onto a stronger setting and moan.

"Make me come, Daddy."

"Make yourself come," he snaps.

I can't help moving, can't help thrusting back onto his cock as the vibrator presses against my clit. I want to do more than submit. I want to fuck him right back. "Oh god, Shane. You feel so good. Oh, *fuck*."

"Say it." He sounds like the devil himself on my shoulder. "You know you want to, baby girl. Say it again."

I don't even hesitate. I'm too out of my mind with pleasure. "I love you!"

He thrusts harder into my ass. "Again."

"*I love you*." And then I'm coming so hard I'm sobbing.

Shane presses me hard down on the vibrator. "Don't stop." He eases out of my ass and I whine even as I shift the setting down to a more rumbling vibration, too needy to stop yet. I listen to him walk into the bathroom. I rub myself on the vibrator, feeling absolutely out of control. My entire being boils down to *more, more, more*.

I don't even hear him come back. One second I'm working on teasing another orgasm from myself and the next I'm flipped onto my back and the vibrator is ripped from my hands. Shane turns it off and tosses it aside. He looks down at me and strokes my throbbing clit with his thumb. "Say it again, Lily."

But I'm not on the edge the same way I was before. I bite my bottom lip. "It doesn't mean anything."

"Don't lie to me." He braces himself over me and rubs the head of his cock over my clit. "We both know it means *everything*."

Fear is almost enough to derail me, but that wicked feeling of the head of his cock against my clit makes it impossible to grasp. "Shane, please."

He pulls me up and fists the fabric of my wadded up dress, using it to guide me to straddle him, facing away. I ease down onto his cock and moan. "This position feels really good."

"I know it does." He keeps a tight hold on my dress, the fabric digging into my skin. "Ride me, Lily. Now."

I move slow, testing out all the angles. And then I look back over my shoulder and find his gaze glued on my ass. "You like what you see."

"I *love* what I see." He urges me up and slams me back down. "Focus. Make yourself come, baby girl. You know you can go again."

I don't even question it. I brace my hands on his big thighs and work myself up and down his cock. "You feel so fucking good. I want you to come and fill me up." I moan. "Fuck, I want you to come all over me."

Shane shifts behind me, sitting up and dragging us back so he can lean against the headboard. He grips my throat lightly with one hand and presses his other to my clit. Not stroking. Letting *me* grind against him each time I move on his cock. "Next time you suck my cock," he growls in my ear. "Next time I'm going to come all over your pretty face. Or maybe I'll come on your breasts."

"Yes." I'm mindlessly working myself onto his cock. More, more, more. I need more. I don't even care. I feel so fucking dirty, so filthy, so fucking *cherished* when I'm with him. I don't understand it, but I can't stop.

I barely register the squeaky step of the stairs. The sound of footsteps in the hallway.

I lean back hard on Shane. I'm so close. So fucking close, and this feels even bigger than the last few. Like it might actually kill me, but what a way to die. "Your cock is so big, Daddy. I'm going to come all over it."

And that's when my ex appears in the doorway. We didn't bother to shut the door when we came upstairs, so he's just *there*. I meet Max's eyes as I'm impaled on his father's cock. I don't know if Shane sees him, but it doesn't matter.

I don't stop.

I hold Max's gaze as I let my orgasm take me. I come so hard, I shriek, my hips jerking and shamelessly rubbing against Shane's hand. Through it all, my ex watches with wide eyes. It's only when I finally slump back against Shane that he curses. "Get the fuck out of here, Max."

Max takes a step back. "Yeah. Uh." His gaze skates over my mostly-naked body like he's never seen me before. "I'm going to go."

Shane lets my dress drop to cover my hips and yanks the straps up over my shoulders. As if Max hasn't seen me naked more times than I can count. "*Out!*" he thunders.

Max finally manages to move, turning and disappearing out of the doorway.

I have the absurd urge to laugh. "Guess we don't need the video after all." I sound strange and tinny to my own ears. This started as a revenge fuck, but actually being caught feels really weird. Not good. Just... I don't even know.

Shane eases me off his cock and tucks himself away. "I'll go talk to him."

That shatters some of my eerie calm. "No, I've got it."

He hesitates. "Lily..."

"I've got it," I repeat. I climb to my feet on shaking legs and head downstairs. I appreciate that Shane wants to take this bullet for me, but I'm the one who initiated this weekend, and I'm an adult. I can handle a conversation with my ex.

Even if it's a conversation while my pussy is still throbbing from fucking his father for two days straight.

I half-expect Max to be gone, but he's standing in the kitchen with his hands braced on the counter. He barely looks at me as I walk through the door. "Are you happy now? Are we even?"

"Are we even? How can you even ask me that?" I wrap my arms around my waist. "How many times did you cheat on me, Max? With how many women?"

His face flushes red. "Look, I'm not proud of that, but you just fucked my dad."

"Yeah. I did."

He looks away. "How am I supposed to know that this didn't start before we broke up?"

Hurt lashes me, flaying away what little guilt I feel. "Because, unlike you, I was faithful. I'm not going to apologize. You hurt me when I found you with her, when you just let me walk away and things ended so shitty. I wanted to hurt you back."

"So you fucked my dad."

I give a vicious little smile. "You're not the only one who calls him Daddy now."

"Jesus, Lily." He shakes his head, looking like he can't decide whether to laugh or start screaming at me. He finally straightens. "You know what? I deserved that."

"Yes, you did."

"I'm sorry." He scrubs a hand over his face. "I *am* sorry. I didn't want things to go like this. I don't know where we got so twisted."

This isn't a conversation to have in Shane's kitchen, but I also want it over. This is the clean break that was denied me for four agonizing days while I waited for Max to call and he never did. Better to have it now and move on with our lives. I lift my chin. "We weren't working. We never should have gotten engaged."

"I know," he says softly, still not quite looking at me. "It just seemed like it was the next logical step. I don't even know if I realized something was missing until I met Jessica and—" He flinches. "It doesn't make what I did right."

"No," I agree. "It doesn't."

His gaze tracks to the ceiling where we can hear Shane's footsteps. "I can't believe you fucked my dad."

I can't believe I want to do *more* than fuck him. I don't say it. It's barely something I'm allowing myself to comprehend. It's sure as hell not something for Max to know one way or another. "I'll box up your stuff and you can pick it up on Friday." I walk to where my purse sits on the counter and dig out the ring. It's a pretty piece of jewelry, but looking at it now, it's just another red flag. I never would have picked out a princess cut on a plain band for myself. "Here."

He stares at it a long time and finally takes it. "You're being remarkably chill right now."

"Max." I wait for him to look at me. "You just found me fucking your father. I think I can afford to be a little chill." It won't last. No matter how clean the break, how necessary, it still hurts. A lot.

He grimaces. "Yeah, well, I'm just not going to think about that too hard." Max hesitates. "Is it just this weekend, or—"

"That's really none of your business."

He opens his mouth, seems to reconsider, and finally nods. "I guess it isn't my business any more, is it?"

"Bring my stuff with you when you come to get your box of shit."

"Sure." He lifts his hands like he wants to hug me and stops. "Fuck, this is weird. I'm sorry. I can't say it enough."

Not sorry enough to have broken up with me like a normal person who's finished with a relationship. Not sorry enough to *talk* to me about how unhappy he obviously was. Not sorry enough stop himself from fucking another woman while he was still engaged to me.

I draw myself up. "I think you should leave now."

"Yeah. Right. Okay." He drags his gaze over me one last time. "See you around, Lily."

"No, Max. You won't." I hold perfectly still as I listen to him walk down the hall and out the front door. I wait a few more moments before I slump against the counter. "Fuck."

Somehow, I keep moving. I walk into the living room and

pick up my phone. It's still recording, which answers the question I hadn't quite been able to bring myself to ask. Shane didn't orchestrate this. It was sheer dumb luck that brought Max here on a morning that started out with us pretending he'd catch us. I give a broken little laugh. "God, I'm so fucked up."

"Lily."

I look up to find that Shane's completely dressed again. He looks down the hallway, and I answer his unspoken question. "He left. I gave him the ring back."

He crosses to me slowly, as if I'm a deer in danger of being spooked. "Are you okay?"

"I got what I wanted, I guess." My chest feels too tight. "Revenge. Except he didn't really care, after his first shock, so it's pretty shitty revenge. He's still going back to her. We're still over. He's not going to be crying over me while he's with his new girlfriend." I hold up a hand before he gets too close. "I know I'm deep in the self-pity stage. Let me have it."

"I didn't say anything." But he has a strange look on his face. "Lily... What if we didn't stop?"

CHAPTER 16

$\mathcal{I}$ shake my head slowly, sure I've heard Shane wrong. "What?"

"Tell me this weekend wasn't the best sex of your life." He takes a step toward me. "Tell me that you didn't enjoy every single second you spent with me." Another step. "Tell me you were lying when you said you loved me."

"Please don't ruin this," I whisper. "We still have one day left."

"That's what I'm saying." He catches my elbows. "What if we had more than one day?" Shane slowly tows me closer until I'm pressed against his chest. "Stay. Give us a shot."

"I've been single for *six days*."

"So?" He skates his hand up my back to dig into my hair and urge my head back so he can kiss the long line of my throat. "Stay."

I'm losing ground and losing it fast. Letting this man get his hands on me was a mistake if I wanted to have enough energy to fight what he's saying. Still, I try. "You can't possibly want to fuck again. Max just caught us."

"And if he was that torn up about it, he'd still be here yelling at us about it."

Fuck, that hurts. "Cruel."

"Logical." Shane keeps kissing my neck. "Come back upstairs, Lily. If you don't want to talk about it today, we won't. We can save it for tomorrow."

I shouldn't. For better or worse, I've accomplished what I set out to do, and staying means something beyond revenge. I can't stay forever. No matter what Shane is offering, eventually he'll come to his senses and then that broken heart chaser will stop being theory and will become my reality.

But I already hurt so much. What's one more day?

I skate my hands up to loop my arms around his neck. "Yes."

He hooks the back of my thighs and lifts me so I can wrap my legs around his waist. Shane carries me back up to his bedroom, and I laugh a little as he shuts and locks the door. He gives me a severe look. "I don't want any more interruptions."

"Me, either." I kiss him.

Shane walks us to the bed and lays me down. "If you were mine, I'd want you only in little dresses like this." He pushes the fabric up just enough to bare my pussy. "You have no idea how crazy it makes me to know that there's nothing stopping me from being inside you."

"Oh yeah?" I prop myself up on my elbows as I watch him strip. I'm not even remotely ashamed to say I give my shoulders a little wiggle so my straps slip off and falls to bare my breasts. "I thought you said I was a little slut for dressing like this."

"You are. *My* little slut." He steps out of his jeans and advances on me. "I'd take you out, Lily. Wherever you want to go. We'd see how long we can last before I'm up your skirt."

"Mmm." I reached down and stroke my pussy. "You going to finger me at dinner, Daddy? Take me into the bathroom and have me for dessert?"

He skates his hands up my thighs, watching me dip a finger into myself. "I ought to bend you over the table and fuck you right there in front of everyone." He squeezes my thighs. "I won't, though. You're just for me, Lily. No one gets to know how sweetly you taste or how pretty you are when you come except for me."

He's claiming me with his words the same way he's previously claimed me with his body. I take a shuddering breath. "Shane—"

"A fantasy." He yanks me to the edge of the mattress. "Let me have my fantasy, baby girl. It's the least you can do since you're leaving me."

"Wait—"

But he talks right over me as he fists his cock and drags it over my pussy. "A thousand fantasies to play out. A million. It'll never be enough." I love how much he loves rubbing the head of his cock over my clit, love how filthy it feels. "I wouldn't even let you wear clothes in the summer. Come home for lunch every day and expect this pussy to be wet and waiting for me. You'll be a good girl and get your pussy ready for your Daddy, won't you, Lily?"

"Yes," I gasp.

"That's right." He dips the head of his cock into me. "And when I come home in the evening, I want you on your knees and ready to suck me down. Take the edge off my day."

Oh god. I want it. I want it so bad, it makes me shake.

He pumps into me slowly, easing in a little more each time. "I won't always finish in that pretty mouth of yours. I'll come on your tits and then eat that pussy until you're screaming so loud the neighbors hear." He sinks even deeper.

"Do you want the neighbors to know what a dirty little slut you are?"

"Yes, Daddy." I fist my hands in the comforter. "I want to ride your mouth while your come is dripping off my nipples."

Shane stills. "Every time I think that mouth of yours can't get filthier, you prove me wrong." He slams the rest of the way into me, making me moan. "What else? Tell me what else you want, baby girl."

I should stay silent, shouldn't play this game with him. It's too seductive to imagine what our life might be like if we didn't have all the obstacles in the way. But with his big cock filling me, I forget all the reasons this is dangerous to my heart. I just want to please him, want to chase the pleasure already building in my body with each thrust. "I want you to take me out to dinner. Eat me out when you pick me up. Take my panties because I'm your dirty little slut." I moan, and he slows down, his expression intent on my face. It takes a few seconds to catch my breath to continue. "And then I want you to fuck me in the parking lot. Fill me up with your come so that it's making a mess of me all through dinner. Every time I move, I'll feel you and know how bad I am."

"That won't be enough for you, though. Will it?" He starts fucking me again, slamming into me over and over again. "You won't be satisfied with two orgasms. The first time I turn around, you'll have your hand up your skirt."

"*Your* hand," I moan. "You put your hand on my knee, and I'll slide it up until you're fucking me with your fingers."

"Better be quiet, baby girl. In a room surrounded by people, you can't come loud and messy like you normally do."

"I will. I promise I will."

Shane leans down and slips an arm around my waist so he can move us fully onto the bed. He kneels between my legs and presses my thighs up and out, opening me obscenely. "Look at how greedy your pussy is for my cock."

Helpless to resist, I look down. His thick length disappears into me again and again. I'm soaked. My pussy, my thighs, his cock. All of it wet with my desire. "So needy," Shane murmurs. "Tell me again how you're finished with this cock, how you'll go the rest of your life without having me inside you again. Tell me you want to walk away."

Something like a sob works its way up my throat. "Shane, please."

"Tell me this wouldn't work, Lily. Tell me that you don't like how you feel when you're with me, when I'm taking care of you. Tell me you don't love me."

A dam breaks inside me and words rush forth. "I *do*. That's the problem. I do like all those things. I *do* love you." My lip won't stop quivering and my eyes burn. "I can't, Shane. It hurts too much. It's too soon. I just… I can't. Please don't make me."

His expression goes tortured and he shifts down to press his body against mine, to gather me as close to him as we can get. He keeps fucking me in slow, languid strokes, his voice rough with emotion. "You don't have to, baby girl. Not until you're ready." He slips an arm beneath my hips, lifting me so his cock can hit a delicious angle inside me. "But when you're ready, Lily? I'm going to be right here. No matter how long it takes." He kisses my neck. "Because I love you, too."

And then there's no more room for words. What else is there to say? We've both laid it out there on the table. There's nothing left but pleasure. We both fight our orgasms, fight finishing this, almost as if we know this is goodbye. It's too good, though. It's always been too good. I come first, clinging to him, milking him with my pussy until he loses control and pounds into me.

Shane barely pulls out of me when his fingers are there,

KATEE ROBERT

spearing into me. "It's not goodbye until morning. Promise me."

"I promise," I gasp.

We devolve into mindless animals. He fingers me while we recover and then hauls me into the bathroom to fuck me in front of the mirror. We barely stop touching in the shower and it starts all over again the second we manage to stumble back into the bedroom, Shane bending me over the bed and eating my pussy and ass until I'm sobbing. He fucks my ass again, whispering filthy possessive things in my ear.

I lose track of how many times I tell him I love him.

No matter how strong our will, our bodies eventually give out and we pass out tangled up in his bed, his hand still cupping my pussy as if trying to milk every last drop of pleasure.

It's one hell of a goodbye.

CHAPTER 17

J wake up before dawn. Every part of my body hurts, but I don't let that stop me as I climb out of bed and stagger to the dress we discarded at some point. I don't know where my black dress is, so this will have to do.

I pause in the doorway and look back, determined to memorize this moment. Shane is sprawled on his back, the sheets bunched around his waist, his broad chest on display. It's almost enough to tempt me back to bed. To pretend our deadline hasn't come. To take him up on everything he's offering me.

I can't.

I just...can't.

"Lily."

I jump. "I didn't realize you were awake."

"I was the moment you moved."

I shift, torn between walking out the door and running back to the bed. "I have to go, Shane. I…"

"It's too soon." He sits up. "You need time to work through your shit."

"Yes." I exhale in something like grief. "It's a lot of shit." It will take longer than seven days to get over this. It's not even getting over *Max* as much as it's getting over the failed relationship. I need time and space to process, but I don't know how long it will take. "I can't ask you to wait for me."

"You don't have to." He drags his hand through his hair. "You're it for me, Lily. I'll wait as long as you need."

My chest aches, but I don't argue. I don't ask him what happens if he's waiting forever. "I'm going to go."

"I'll walk you out."

"No." I take a quick step back, even though he's barely shifted. "If you get up, I'm going to second-guess myself and then I'll end up on your cock again. Which means we'll be having an identical conversation next time we surface."

He curses softly. "Text me when you get home."

I don't tell him that even that much communication is probably crossing a line. "I will." I pause. "Do you want the videos?"

Shane holds my gaze. "Only when you're ready to start again. Send them to me when you're ready to be mine, baby girl."

"Yes, Daddy," I whisper.

And then I flee.

CHAPTER 18

FEBRUARY

5:48pm

Shane: How are you holding up?
Me: It's been rough.
Shane: What can I do?
Me: I just need time, I think.
Shane: Take all the time you need, Lily. I mean it.

CHAPTER 19

APRIL

1:13am
   Me: I want to fuck.
   Shane: Lily, are you drunk?
   Me: Maybe. Girl's night!
   Me: But they're gone and I want my Daddy's cock.
   Shane: Where are you?
   Me: The Silver Spoon.
   Shane: Give me fifteen minutes.
   Shane: Do not *leave with anyone.*
   Me: I only want to leave with you.

2:01 am
   Me: I am so mad at you.
   Shane: You won't be tomorrow.
   Me: You turned me down!
   Shane: You're drunk, baby girl.
   Shane: You'd regret fucking me.
   Me: You're an asshole.
   Shane: Guess I'll have to live with that.

. . .

10:26 am

> *Me: I'm sorry.*
> *Shane: How are you feeling?*
> *Me: Like I'm dying.*
> *Me: I'm never drinking again.*
> *Me: I shouldn't have text you.*
> *Shane: You can always call me for a ride.*
> *Shane: I'd rather you be safe.*
> *Me: Thanks. For everything.*
> *Shane: Any time, Lily.*

CHAPTER 20

MAY

3 : 52pm
     Me: I saw you today.
Shane: Oh?
Me: Yeah, pulling out of the store parking lot.
Shane: Sorry I missed you.
Me: Me too.
Me: I do.
Me: Miss you.
Shane: I miss you, too.
Me: I just need more time.
Shane: Take as long as you need.
Me: You keep saying that, but you won't wait forever.
Shane: Let me worry about that.

CHAPTER 21

JUNE

I don't know how it happens. One day, I'm still struggling to stay afloat, the pressure easing a little with each week that passes. The next I wake up determined to start living again. I *hate* that it took me six months to work through this, but every time I felt like the ground might be steadying under my feet, something would happen.

So I keep my head down and focus entirely on work until the end of the school year. And then summer vacation starts and I feel... Okay. Better than okay. Almost like myself again.

I miss Shane so much, it's like I actually carved out my heart that weekend and left it behind in his house. No matter how much an asshole I act, he's been a goddamn saint since. Never pushing me. Never trying to play dirty. Just patient and understanding and I am so done with all my bullshit.

It's time to move forward. I finally feel ready.

The fact that it's an unseasonal blistering hot June day only seems to spur me on. Like I've been standing still for so long, treading water, and now I'm ready to sprint. There's only one direction for me to sprint to: Shane.

If he'll still have me.

I pick up my phone and flick through to my secret folder where I keep the videos from that weekend. I've watched them more times than I care to admit. Bringing myself to orgasm at the sight of his fingers in my pussy or me riding his mouth, riding his cock. My hands are nowhere near as good as the real thing.

He said to send the videos when I'm finally ready to move forward.

My thumb hovers over the button to do it, but I hesitate. Is it too late? Have I lingered too long? Nervous energy has me texting him instead.

Me: It's wicked hot today.

He responds almost immediately.

Shane: I was actually thinking of getting the pool ready to go.

Just like that, an idea forms. A filthy, perfect idea.

Me: You should. Gotta maximize every hot summer day.

Shane: Agreed.

Me: Are you still going home for lunch?

Shane: Sometimes. Why?

Me: Just wondering.

Me: I have to go. I'll catch up with you soon.

Shane: Okay. Have a good day.

I check the clock. It's mid-morning, which means I don't have much time. I take a shower and get ready, throwing on a pair of shorts and a tank top and filling a tote bag with the things I'll need. It's not until I'm driving to Shane's that my nerves ramp up.

If he doesn't want me anymore, I'm setting myself up for one hell of a humiliating experience.

I find the spare key exactly where it's always been, tucked under a fake rock near the front door, and let myself in. Even though I know better, I drift through the house. I'm not exactly looking for evidence that he's moved on, but I still exhale in relief when I find things exactly as they were the last time I was here.

It's game time.

I strip and pull on the white wrap cover-up that I bought a month ago because it made me think of Shane. The cut almost looks Grecian, narrow swathes of fabric draping from my shoulders over my breasts and crisscrossing at my hips to form a tiny little skirt. It's cute with my swimsuit on under it. It's dirty as hell without.

I take a deep breath and walk out into the backyard. The cover is still on the pool, but he's got the lounge chairs out like I hoped. Shane likes to read in the evenings out here as soon as the weather's nice, so I bet he brought them out of storage the second the temperature edged to barely tolerable.

I drape myself over the lounge chair in the shade and take a deep breath. Here we go. I lift my phone, position it over my face in a selfie angle, and push record. "Hi Shane. I might have done a little breaking and entering to get into your backyard, but is it really breaking and entering if I know where the spare key is?"

I'm talking too fast, my words tumbling over themselves, but I can't seem to stop. "I didn't expect to be this nervous, but here we are." I nibble my bottom lip. "I know you said to send those videos when I was ready, but I don't want to live in the past. I want a future." I give a small smile. "So I'm making you a new video."

I drag my finger down my neck, carefully following it with the camera, to cup my left breast. The white fabric is almost see-through. "I bought this just for you." I tug it to the side, baring my breast, and let my fingers linger on my nipple. "I hope you like it."

It's harder to get this angle right. I have to sit up a bit as I pull up the wrap to show him my pussy. "Oops. No panties. I

121

know how much you hate that." I part my pussy and drag my middle finger up my center. "I've missed you, Daddy. I can't wait for you to fill me up again." I shift the camera back to my face, but I don't stop touching myself. "Want to come home and have me for lunch?" I blow him a kiss and end the video.

I almost chicken out before sending it. But I've come too far to back out now.

My phone rings sixty seconds later.

Shane.

I'm shaking as I answer. "Hello?"

"Baby girl." He sounds quiet and almost furious. "Are you fingering yourself in my backyard right now?"

Just like that, my nerves disappear. He wouldn't call me that if he wasn't one hundred percent in on this. I recline against the lounge chair and go back to leisurely stroking my clit. "Yes, Daddy."

His breathing shudders out. "Don't stop. I'll be there in fifteen minutes." His voice goes hard. "Don't you dare come. That orgasm is mine and I intend to take it."

"Better hurry then." I hang up to the sound of his cursing.

For all my teasing, I don't really want to come before he gets here. But that doesn't stop me from stoking my need higher with every touch. I debate taking off the cover-up, but it feels too good to stop, so I don't bother.

Exactly fourteen minutes after we hung up, I hear the front door slam.

Shane stalks outside and stops short, like he can't believe I'm really here. The shock on his face only lasts a moment, but it's delicious. He's wearing a suit without a tie, the top two buttons undone. As I watch, he shrugs out of the jacket and sets it on the back of the second lounge chair.

I give my clit another circle and hold my breath. Are we playing or are we going to talk?

He doesn't make me wait long. "Tell me something."

"Yes?"

He glances at the clear blue sky and then down at me. "You're out here mostly naked and you haven't put on any sunscreen, have you?"

"Um." My skin heats. "No."

"Thought so." He disappears into the house for a few minutes and comes back with a tube of the stuff. Shane stalks to me and makes an impatient motion with his hand. "Sit up."

I obey, reluctantly removing my hand from my clit. "Sorry, Daddy."

"You will be if you get burned." He eyes me and yanks down my cover-up to pool at my waist. "Jesus, baby girl. You aren't even trying." Before I can respond, he squirts some sunscreen into his palm and starts spreading it onto my skin. His hands shake a little as he starts at my shoulders and coasts his hands down my arms, but that's okay. I'm shaking too. It's been six long months since he touched me and I have to bite my bottom lip to keep from begging him not to stop.

I expect him to rush through this to get to the good parts. I should know better by now. I really should.

Shane massages the sunscreen into my arms, going slow to ensure he doesn't miss a spot. Only once he's satisfied does he urge me to lay back and start in on my upper chest and breasts. Neither of us say a word, not when he lightly pinches my nipples. Not when he leans down and nibbles at the underside of my breasts. His big hands bracket my ribs. "Lift your hips."

I obey instantly, and he drags the cover-up down my body and drops it onto the ground. He holds my gaze. "It doesn't cover you worth a damn, so we're going to make sure we get every inch before you put it back on."

I lick my lips. "Yes, Daddy."

He rubs lotion into my stomach and hip and lower to the top of my mound, before bypassing my pussy entirely and giving my legs the same thorough attention he's given the rest of me. "Turn over."

"But—"

"Don't make me ask again."

I sigh and roll onto my stomach. Shane starts at my shoulders and works his way down. Slow. Agonizingly slowly. He palms my ass, squeezing and parting me, and his breath shudders out. "Fuck, you're even more perfect than I remember."

"Touch me. Please."

"Mmm." He wipes his hand on the towel under me. "That should do it. Get back on your back."

I flip over and start to sit up, but Shane's hand in the center of my chest stops me. He looks serious and almost forbidding. "I'm not playing games with you this time, baby girl. You part those legs and let me in, I'm keeping you. You don't get to say you need space and walk away from me again. This pussy will be mine."

"Can I tell you a secret?" I wrap my hands around his wrist and drag his hand slowly down my body. "This pussy has been yours since you fingered me on your couch." He lets me guide a single finger into me. I whimper a little. It's been so long.

"What are you saying?" His brows lower and his hand tenses beneath mine. "Use your words, Lily. I know you know how."

"There's been no one else." I arch my hips up a little, working myself on his finger. "No one's stuck their hands into my panties. No tongues have played with my clit. I haven't ridden any cocks. No one's touched me since you."

"Put your hands above your head and grip the chair."

I eagerly obey. "Six long months," he muses, pumping his finger into me slowly. "Would you like a secret in return?"

"Yes."

He wedges a second finger into me. "I haven't fucked anyone, either." He catches my chin with his free hand, his fingers digging in until I gasp. "I haven't let another set of lips wrap around my cock. I haven't stuck my hand up any short skirts to finger anyone."

I moan and lift my hips. "I've been going crazy with wanting you. I watched those videos so many times."

"Your panties are in my nightstand." He leans down and licks the shell of my ear. "I've jacked myself with them so many times, I feel like a dirty old man."

I like the picture he paints. Of my white lace panties bunched in his hand as he wraps it around his big cock. "That's hot."

"Not as hot as the feeling of your pussy clamped around my fingers." He exhales slowly and withdraws his fingers. "We should go inside before we scandalize the neighbors."

"You're right." I run my hands down my body, already shaking with need. "But don't you want a taste, Daddy? Just a little taste before we move."

He makes a sound like he's in pain. "Just as much a dirty little slut as ever."

"I miss your mouth. I miss it so much, I think I might die if you don't give me your tongue right now."

"Did I tell you to stop holding the chair?"

Instantly, I lift my arms over my head and grip the chair. "Sorry."

"Spoiled." He moves to wedge himself between my thighs. "Needy." He exhales against my clit. "Demanding."

I stare down my body as he parts my pussy. Behind him, I see movement in a window on the other side of the fence. "Your neighbors are watching," I whisper.

"That's what you want, isn't it, baby girl? You're naked in my backyard, tits on full display, your pussy practically weeping for me. You want them to look." He inhales slowly. "Is it that bastard Richard?"

I have to struggle not to lift my hips, not to close that last little bit of distance between us. "Yes." I don't raise my voice. "He's standing in his window."

"Probably wishing he was in my position right now, about to taste your pretty pussy." He urges my thighs wider. "You're going to put on a show for him, aren't you, baby girl? Let him know exactly how good your Daddy makes you feel."

CHAPTER 22

Shane finally, *finally* dips his head down and makes contact. Our moans mingle at the first swipe of his tongue. I can't take my eyes off him, off the bliss on his face as he tongues my pussy. My breasts are heaving with each inhale and I know we paint a sinful picture, him fully clothed with his head between my thighs, me naked and splayed, fully on display. "Do you think he wants to fuck me, Daddy?" I'm fighting to hold still, to not thrash as he tongues me. "Do you think he wants to sink into my tight pussy and watch my breasts shake as I bounce on his cock?"

Shane plasters one hand on my lower stomach and lifts his head to glare at me. "Yes, Lily, that's exactly what I think he wants."

I risk letting go of the lounge chair and sink my hands into his silvering hair. It's a little longer than the last time he had me in this position. "Too bad." I lift my hips and rub myself against his mouth. It feels even filthier because he doesn't move. He just holds still and lets me grind on him like the dirty little slut I am. "Too bad," I repeat. "This pussy is just for you."

And then his mouth is on me and this time he stops playing around. He whips us both into a frenzy, sucking and licking me until I'm panting and a faint sheen of sweat rises from my skin. "Oh god, I'm going to come."

"No, you're not." He pulls me up and reverses our positions, dropping onto the lounge chair and settling me astride him. "Take out my cock. You want to come, you come on my dick."

I undo his pants with trembling hands and draw his cock out. He's even bigger than I remember and I bite my bottom lip as I stroke him. "You want me to let you inside with no condom, Daddy?" I hold him steady and rub myself against his length. "You want me to ride you bare?"

"Get on my cock, Lily. Don't make me tell you again."

I brace one hand on his shoulder and guide him to my entrance. "Fuck, you're so big." I writhe a little as I try to take him deeper. "I forgot how big you are."

"So fucking tight," Shane mutters. He grips my hips, pressing me down, ever down.

I gasp. "It's too much."

"No it's not." He doesn't stop, just keeps working me on his cock. "You're going to take every inch, because you're a good girl and that's what good girls do. They take their Daddy's cocks to the hilt." And then, impossibly, I do.

I rest my forehead against his as he keeps me pinned down onto him, not letting either of us move. "I missed you so much. Not just this. You."

"I missed you, too, Lily." He shifts his head a little and then his mouth is on mine. Shane kisses me like he owns me, like he never doubted for a second that I'd make my way back to him. He kisses me like he'll never get enough.

Finally, finally, he breaks the kiss. "Now ride my cock. Show everyone watching what a good girl you are."

I reach behind me and brace my hands on his thighs. I

don't care if the entire neighborhood is watching. All that matters is the way Shane looks at me. He runs his hands up and down the front of my body. Cupping my breasts. Playing with my nipples. Circling my clit. Driving my desire higher and higher with each touch. He finally rests his thumb against my clit, letting me grind against that contact point. "Are you trying to hold out, Lily?"

"Maybe," I moan.

"You're trying to deny me that orgasm that's mine by right." He pulls me off his cock and the next thing I know, I'm face-down on the lounge chair with my ass in the air. Shane guides my feet to the ground, lifting my ass farther. "Just for that, I'm going to make you come until I get tired of eating your pretty pussy, and then I'm going to fuck your ass. You have a problem with that?"

"No, Daddy!"

"That's what I fucking thought." He spreads me and then his mouth is there, eating me out from behind. I have no idea if the guy across the fence is still watching, but the thought that he might be only ramps my desire hotter. Shane sucks on my clit and then fucks me with his tongue, finally moving up to work my ass. Before starting it all over again. It doesn't take long before my legs are shaking and I'm clinging to the chair. "I'm close."

"Fuck yes, you are. You're going to come all over my face." He doesn't stop, he doesn't slow down. He just drags the first orgasm out of me as if it truly is his by right. Shane holds me still as I shudder and writhe against his face. He chuckles darkly. "That's a good start."

My eyes fly open. "Shane—"

But he's not listening. He starts tonguing me again, ruthlessly winding me up. It might have been six months since he had his mouth on me, but he hasn't forgotten exactly what I need to get off. The second orgasm hits like a freight train and my legs give out. Shane barely catches me before I hit the chair, and he wastes no time scooping me into his arms. "That's enough of a show for now. He'll have to imagine the rest."

He stalks into the house, and I blink in the seeming darkness after being in the sun. "I can't believe you just did that."

"Six months, Lily. I've had six months of wanting you and being denied. I'd fuck you right in the middle of the street if that's where I found you today."

He takes the stairs two at a time and walks into the bedroom. Shane sets me on my feet and releases me. "Get on the bed. Show me how good I made that pussy feel."

I scramble onto the bed and spread my legs. "So good, Daddy." I part my pussy as he strips, his gaze on me. "See how good? I'm so wet from coming, so ready for your cock."

Shane slips his phone out of his pocket and sets it on the bed, and then takes off his pants. "I'm going to take a picture of you, Lily. In fact, I'm going to take several."

It's not quite a question, but I'm already nodding. "Yes, do it."

He lifts his phone and snaps one. Then he moves in closer. "You can do better than that. Wider." I whimper and obey, spreading my pussy lips. "Good girl," he mutters and the camera on the phone clicks again. "Up."

I sit up and gasp when he grips my chin. "Did you wear this pink lipstick for me?"

I nod as much as I can. "You said you wanted to see my pretty pink lips wrap around your cock."

The expression in his dark eyes is devastating. "Open." He holds the phone steady as he eases his cock into my mouth. "That's right, baby girl. Suck me."

I moan and work to take him deeper. Over and over again, until he tosses the phone to the side and brackets my head with his hands, easing me off his cock. "You've got to stop if you want me to last."

"Maybe I want you to come on my tits."

Shane curses and gives me a gentle push to have me flop onto my back. "We have time." Except he's not looking at me like we have time. He's looking at me like I'm a feast laid out for his benefit and he doesn't know where to start. He finally kneels between my thighs and pushes two fingers into me. "Your ass is mine later. I need your pussy right now."

"Yes, Daddy."

He moves to sit with his back against the headboard and motions me over. "Come here. Face away from me."

As I obey, I'm slammed with the memory of what happened last time we were in this exact position. He even left the door open. "Are you sure?"

"Yes." He guides his cock into me and I sink down until he's sheathed completely. Just like last time, Shane presses one hand to my pussy and brackets my throat with the other. "Did you think I didn't notice?"

I start riding him slowly, up and down his cock, rubbing myself against his hand. "Notice what?"

"You didn't stop when he walked in." He kisses my shoulder. "You looked right at him and rode me until you came."

Six months has taken the sting out of my breakup. Without all the emotional baggage, there's only heat left to play this out. "It felt too good to stop," I murmur. "I didn't care if he was watching. I needed to come all over my Daddy's cock."

"You like being watched, don't you, Lily?" He nips my earlobe. "You like it when I fuck you in the kitchen because the neighbors might see. You like it in the backyard for the same reason. It's why you're naked and playing with your pussy by the pool every chance you get."

I grind down hard on his cock. "*Yes.*" I moan. I lick my

lips. "You love it, too." I ride him faster. "You loved fingering my pussy while you waved at the neighbors. And putting that plug in my ass in the parking lot. And fucking me in your truck. You can't get enough of my pussy, can you, Daddy?"

"I can't get enough of *you*." His fingers flex on my throat. Not enough to do anything but remind me of how much bigger he is, how much more powerful. "We should stop," he rumbles. "I think I hear someone coming up the stairs."

Even though it's pretend, I moan loud and long. "I don't care. I can't stop."

"Walking down the hallway."

"I'm so close, Daddy. Don't make me stop."

"Don't stop. Don't you dare fucking stop."

And then I'm coming, crying out and slumping back against him. He topples me onto my stomach and goes to his knees behind me. Shane grips my hips and yanks me back as he thrusts forward, impaling me on his cock. "I'm feeling generous because you orgasmed so sweetly. Where do you want my come, baby girl?"

"My breasts. All over them."

He flips me onto my back and drives into me. Shane treats me like I'm a precious fuck toy, and I can't get enough. As his strokes start to go wild, he pulls out and shift up my body. He jerks his cock roughly, and I flinch as he comes across my breasts in hot spurts. Shane keeps stroking, like he's determined to empty every last drop onto me.

I look down at myself. "That's so hot."

"Dirty little slut," he murmurs and drags a single finger over my nipple, smearing himself over me. I don't get a chance to do more than moan before he moves down and starts licking my pussy again.

I whimper. "You're going to be late going back to work."

"Give me a little fucking credit, Lily. I took the rest of the day off. I have no obligations this afternoon except making you come enough to start balancing the scales for the last six months."

I stare at him with wide eyes. "What?"

"You heard me." Shane gives me a long lick. "You said it yourself. This pussy has been mine since January. That means I'm owed." He sucks lightly on my clit. "You teach math, baby girl. If I gave you two orgasms on weekdays and six on weekends, what's that balance out to?" He goes back to licking my pussy.

"I can't think when you do that."

He spears his tongue into me once, twice, a third time. "I have faith you can figure it out."

I'm covered in his come and his mouth is working my clit and he wants me to do *math*. "Shane, please."

"Don't make me wait, Lily."

My breath sobs out as I try to obey. I should be able to do this problem in seconds, but it takes me several long minutes of him eating me out to finally blurt, "Five hundred and twenty-eight. Ish."

"Five hundred and twenty-eight. And your normal daily orgasms don't count." He nuzzles me. "Sounds like I have a lot of ground to cover."

My laugh sounds a little hysterical. "I hope you don't think you can make that up today. I know we agreed that we probably won't die from coming too much, but you might make liars out of us."

"Not today." He leverages one of my legs up and back, leaving me wide open for him. "I'm keeping you, Lily. I have a lifetime to make them up, and I plan to use every single fucking day."

He goes down on me until I stop being able to form words, until he teases so many orgasms out of me, I lose count. Then Shane flips me over and fucks me again with his thumb in my ass. It's just a tease for what will come later, and as much of a happy little slut I am, even in the middle of being driven mindless by him, I'm aware that I can't just take his cock in my ass without being prepped. No matter how much I want to.

At some point we make it into the shower, and then back to the bed, but it's a little hazy. All I know is that I wake up the next morning with Shane's tongue in my pussy.

I moan and dig my hands into his hair. "You're setting a dangerous precedent."

"Mmm." He drags me down beneath him and guides his cock into me. "Morning."

"Morning." I wrap my legs around his waist. "I've been waiting for a moment where we aren't fucking to say something, but I don't think we're going to get there anytime soon."

He slips an arm under my hips to lift them for a superior angle. "You have a point."

I cup his face in my hands. "I love you. I meant it when I said it in January, and I mean it now."

"I love you, too." He kisses me, long and hard, as he fucks me. Shane shifts down to growl in my ear. "Don't freak out."

My orgasm is already approaching and I hook my feet around his thighs to get better leverage to lift my hips to meet his thrusts. "Freak out?"

"Because if you try to bolt again, I'm liable to hunt you down and fuck you wherever I find you to remind you who you belong to."

I shiver. "Just say it."

He leans back and pins my hips to the bed, fucking me hard enough to make my breasts bounce with each stroke. "I'm going to marry you, Lily. You're going to be my wife and my baby girl and I'm going to worship this pussy every single fucking day for the rest of our lives."

His words push me over the edge as much as his cock does. "Yes, I'll marry you. *Yes, yes, yes.*"

It's only a little later, when we're tangled together and trying to relearn how to breathe, that I start laughing. Shane leverages himself up on one arm and looks down at me. "What's so funny?"

"I guess you were right before." I lean up and kiss his throat, tumbling him onto his back. "You're fucking me, you're going to date me, and eventually you're going to make me Max's stepmom." I try to still my laughter, but don't quite manage it. "Do you think he'll call me Mom?"

Shane shakes his head in mock disappointment. "There goes your mouth again." He wraps my hair around his fist and urges me down his body. "Guess I'll have to find a way to occupy it so you don't get into trouble, won't I, baby girl?"

I lick up his length and then back down again. "Yes, Daddy."

* * *

THANK you so much for reading this dirty little book. I had a blast writing it, and I hope it provided you with an escape just like it provided me while I drafted it.

Want to stay up to date on my new releases, including any upcoming A Touch of Taboo novels? Sign up for my newsletter!

Looking for your next sexy read? You can pick up my MMF ménage THEIRS FOR THE NIGHT, my FREE novella that features an exiled prince, his bodyguard, and the bartender they can't quite manage to leave alone.

ACKNOWLEDGMENTS

This book feels extra collaborative, because it was written so quickly and because the support it got when it was still in the idea stages is the reason I started writing. If you saw that tweet or instagram post and went YES, thank you! You gave me the push to just do the damn thing.

Thank you to Amy Ball for both series and book title suggestions. They're perfect!

Big thanks to Nikke Sloane for writing such an outstanding series that sold me on being into father-in-laws. If you haven't read the Filthy Rich American series, I cannot recommend it enough!

Thank you to Piper J Drake and Asa Maria Bradley for being there while I was in the midst of writing this.

Big thanks to Jenny Nordback, Nisha Sharma, and Andie J Christopher for giving me a big thumbs up and DO THE DAMN THING throughout drafting. I appreciate you!

As always, thanks to Tim. This time for not blinking when I'm like "So I'm writing this book about a woman who fucks her former father-in-law." Of course you are, babe. LOL. Love you!

ABOUT THE AUTHOR

Katee Robert is a *New York Times* and USA Today bestselling author of contemporary romance and romantic suspense. *Entertainment Weekly* calls her writing "unspeakably hot." Her books have sold over a million copies. She lives in the Pacific Northwest with her husband, children, a cat who thinks he's a dog, and two Great Danes who think they're lap dogs.

Website: www.kateerobert.com

Made in the USA
Middletown, DE
05 November 2024

63906070R00090